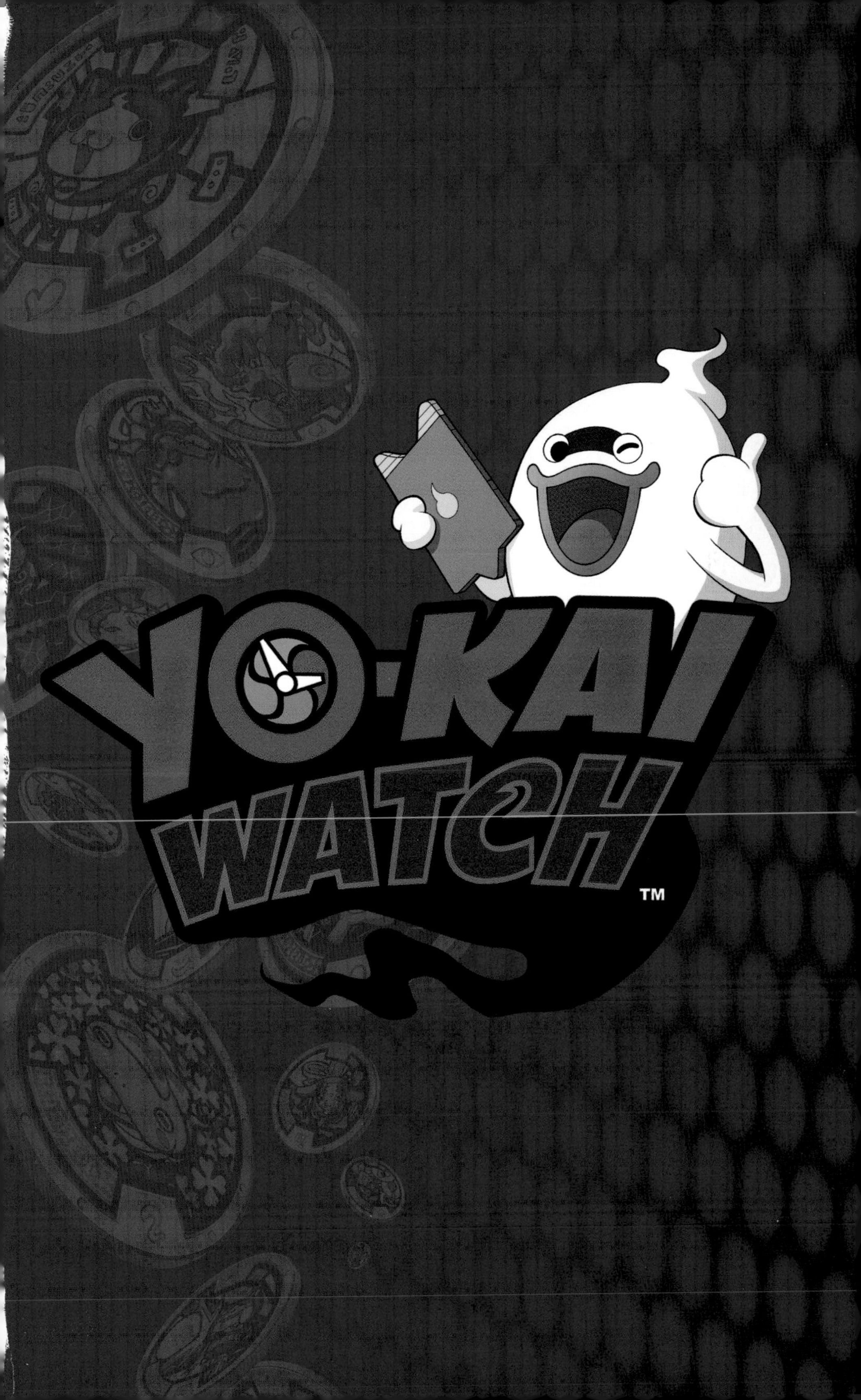
YO-KAI
WATCH
TM

Become our fan on Facebook **facebook.com/idwpublishing**

Follow us on Twitter **@idwpublishing**

Subscribe to us on YouTube **youtube.com/idwpublishing**

See what's new on Tumblr **tumblr.idwpublishing.com**

Check us out on Instagram **instagram.com/idwpublishing**

Ted Adams, CEO & Publisher
Greg Goldstein, President & COO
Robbie Robbins, EVP/Sr. Graphic Artist
Chris Ryall, Chief Creative Officer
David Hedgecock, Editor-in-Chief
Laurie Windrow, Senior Vice President of Sales & Marketing
Matthew Ruzicka, CPA, Chief Financial Officer
Lorelei Bunjes, VP of Digital Services
Jerry Bennington, VP of New Product Development

ISBN: 978-1-63140-993-6   21   20   19   18   2   3   4   5

Originally published as YO-KAI WATCH issues #1–3.

WRITER:
ERIC M. ESQUIVEL

ARTIST:
TINA FRANSCISCO

COLORIST:
MAE HAO

LETTERER:
CHRISTA MIESNER

ASSISTANT EDITORS:
DAVID MARIOTTE AND
CHASE MAROTZ

SERIES EDITOR:
DAVID HEDGECOCK

COVER ARTIST:
ROB DUENAS

COLLECTION EDITORS:
JUSTIN EISINGER AND
ALONZO SIMON

COLLECTION DESIGNER:
CHRISTA MIESNER

PUBLISHER:
TED ADAMS

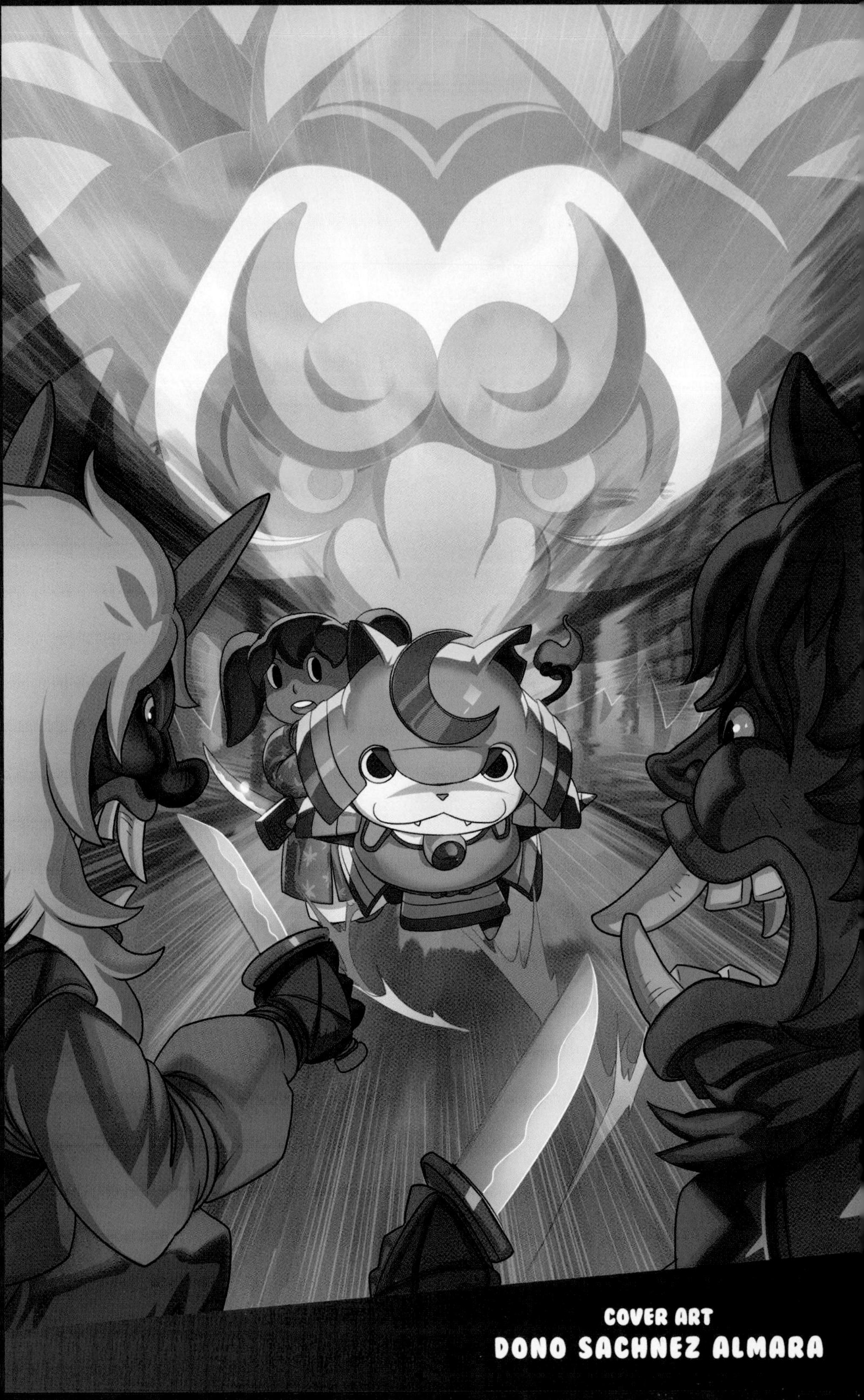

COVER ART
DONO SACHNEZ ALMARA

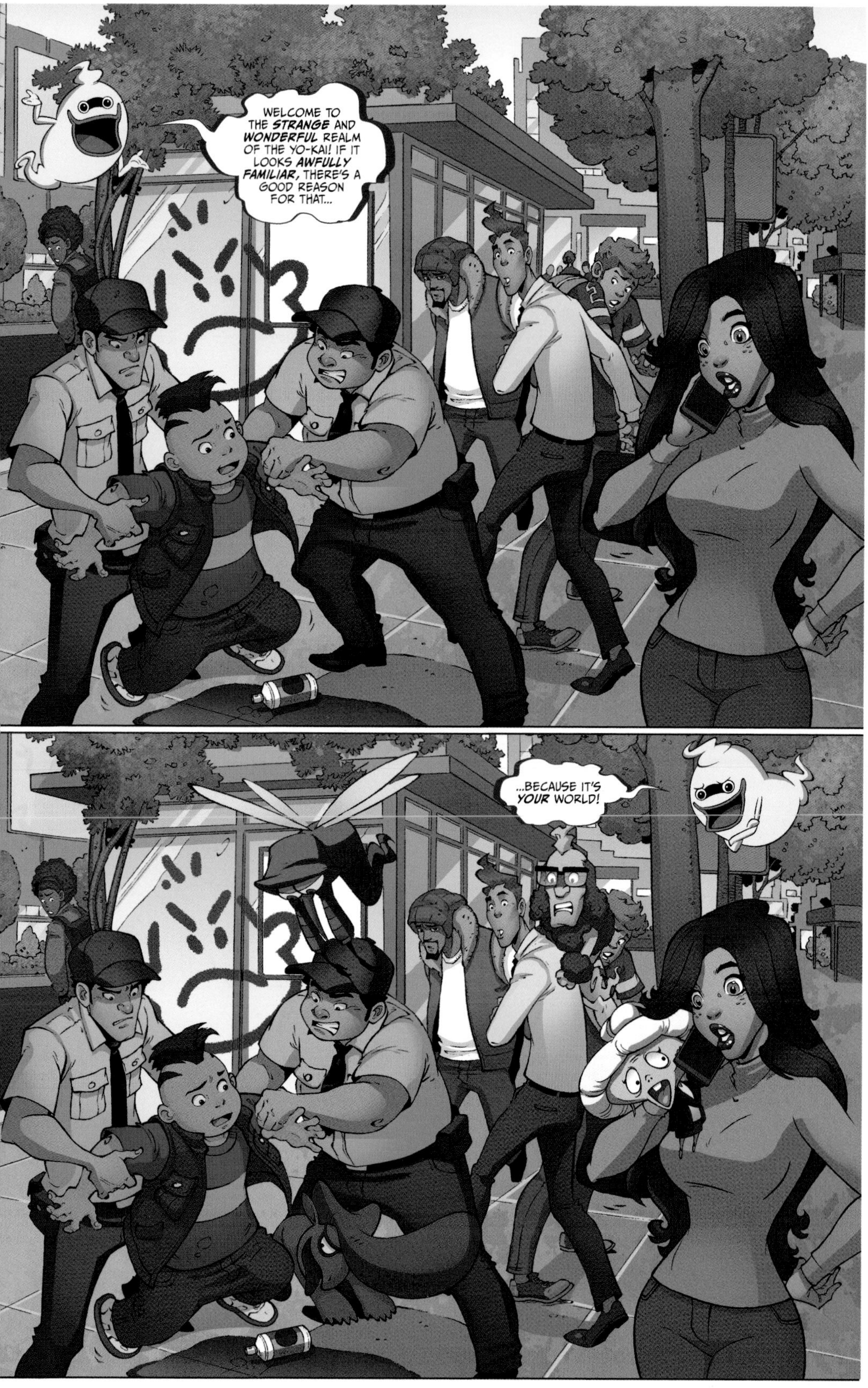
WELCOME TO THE STRANGE AND WONDERFUL REALM OF THE YO-KAI! IF IT LOOKS AWFULLY FAMILIAR, THERE'S A GOOD REASON FOR THAT...
...BECAUSE IT'S YOUR WORLD!

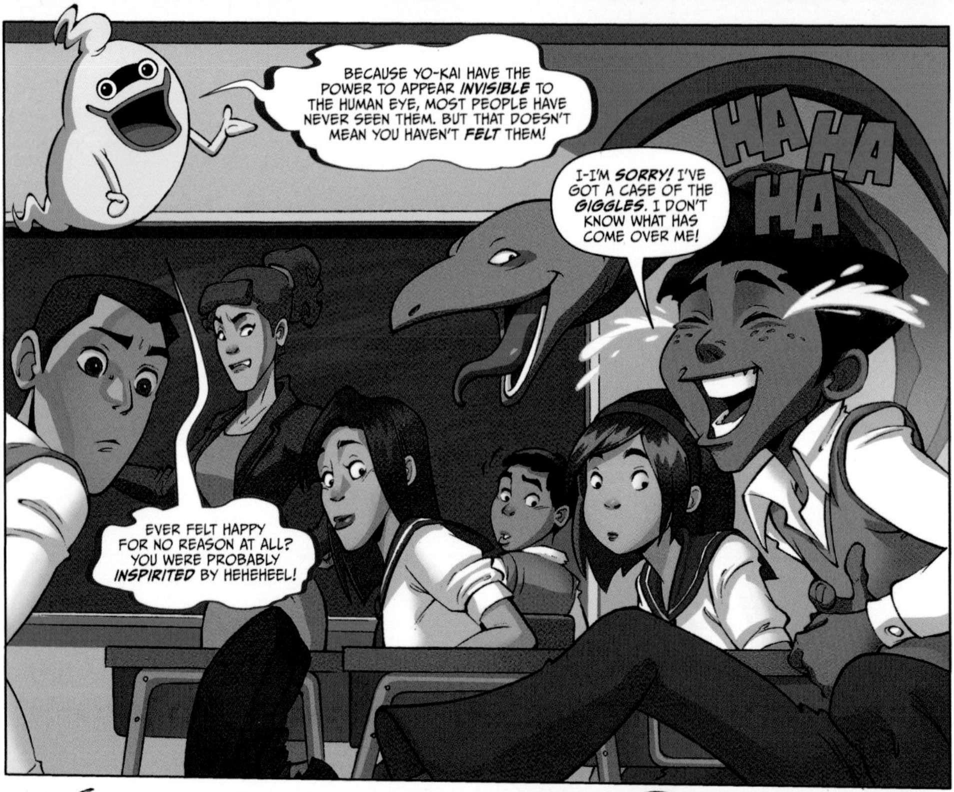
BECAUSE YO-KAI HAVE THE POWER TO APPEAR INVISIBLE TO THE HUMAN EYE, MOST PEOPLE HAVE NEVER SEEN THEM. BUT THAT DOESN'T MEAN YOU HAVEN'T FELT THEM!
HAHAHA
I-I'M SORRY! I'VE GOT A CASE OF THE GIGGLES. I DON'T KNOW WHAT HAS COME OVER ME!
EVER FELT HAPPY FOR NO REASON AT ALL? YOU WERE PROBABLY INSPIRITED BY HEHEHEEL!

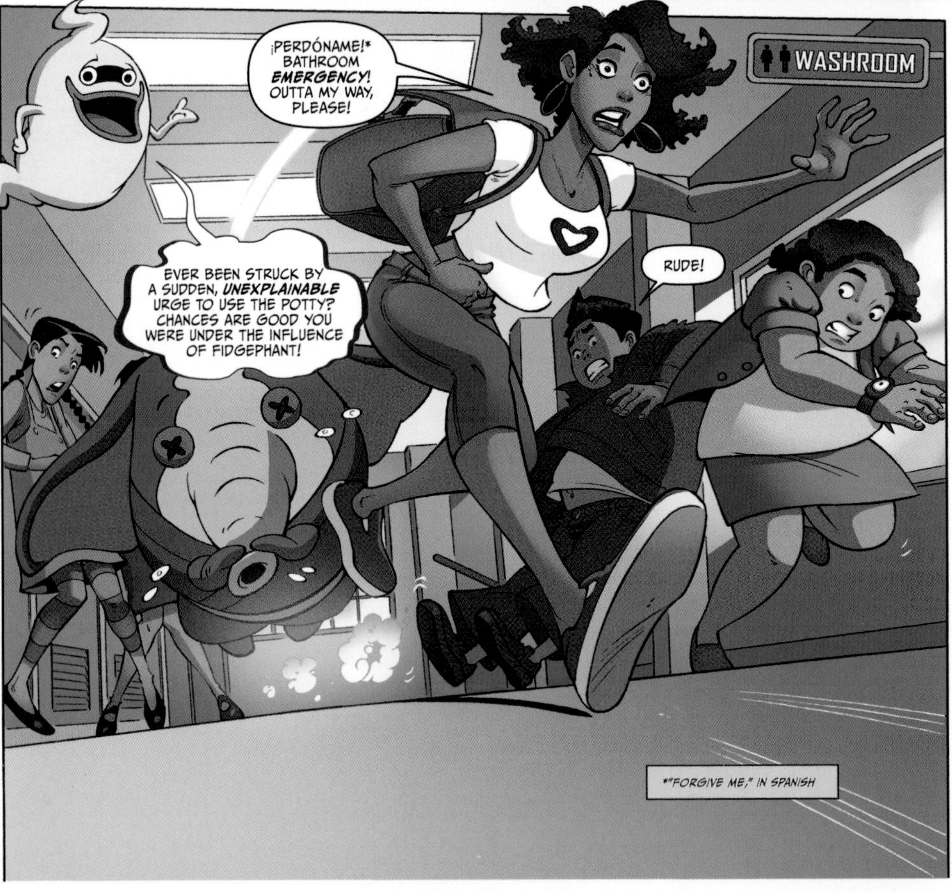
¡PERDÓNAME!* BATHROOM EMERGENCY! OUTTA MY WAY, PLEASE!
WASHROOM
EVER BEEN STRUCK BY A SUDDEN, UNEXPLAINABLE URGE TO USE THE POTTY? CHANCES ARE GOOD YOU WERE UNDER THE INFLUENCE OF FIDGEPHANT!
RUDE!
*"FORGIVE ME," IN SPANISH

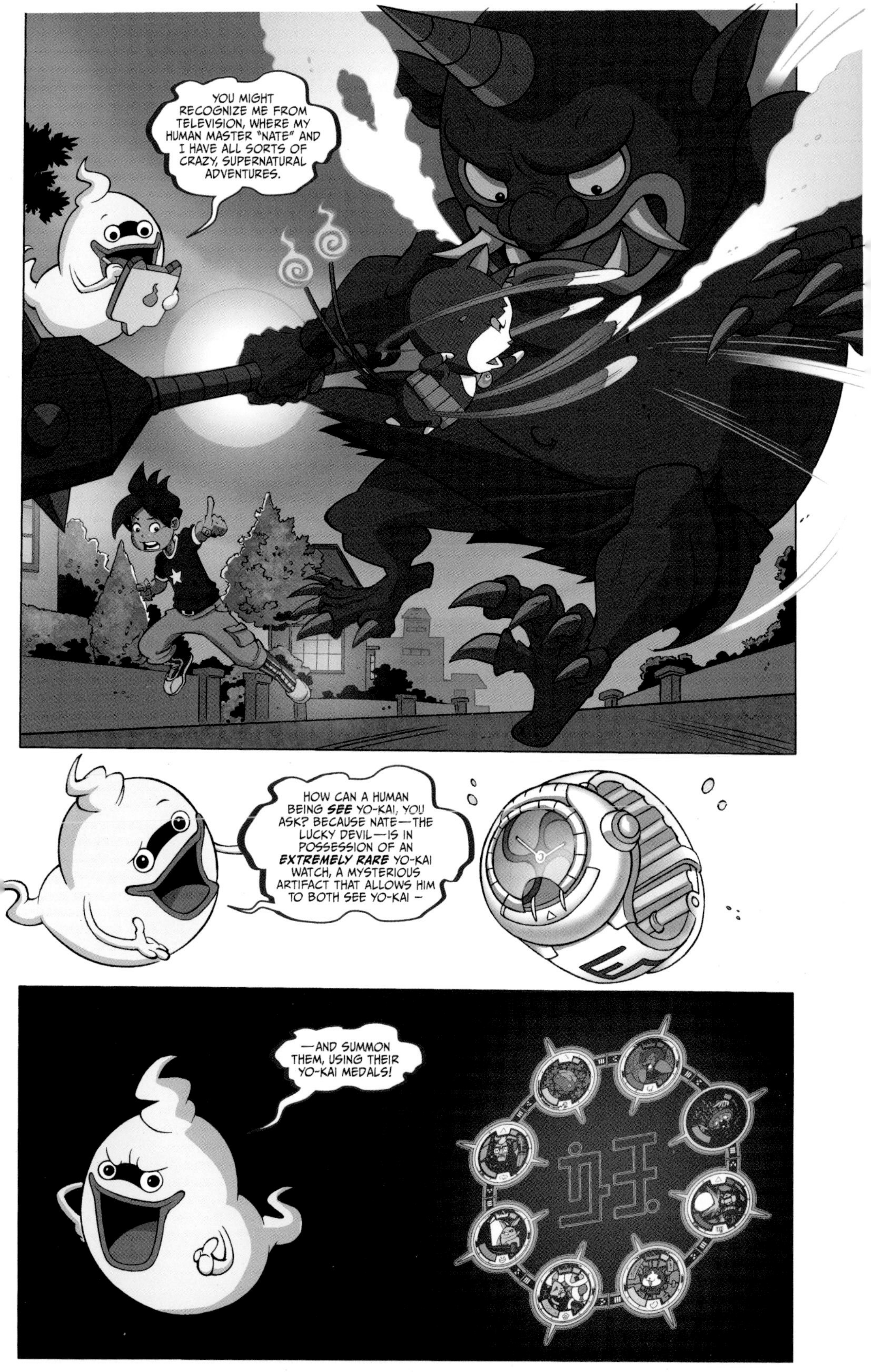
YOU MIGHT RECOGNIZE ME FROM TELEVISION, WHERE MY HUMAN MASTER "NATE" AND I HAVE ALL SORTS OF CRAZY, SUPERNATURAL ADVENTURES.
HOW CAN A HUMAN BEING SEE YO-KAI, YOU ASK? BECAUSE NATE—THE LUCKY DEVIL—IS IN POSSESSION OF AN EXTREMELY RARE YO-KAI WATCH, A MYSTERIOUS ARTIFACT THAT ALLOWS HIM TO BOTH SEE YO-KAI –
—AND SUMMON THEM, USING THEIR YO-KAI MEDALS!

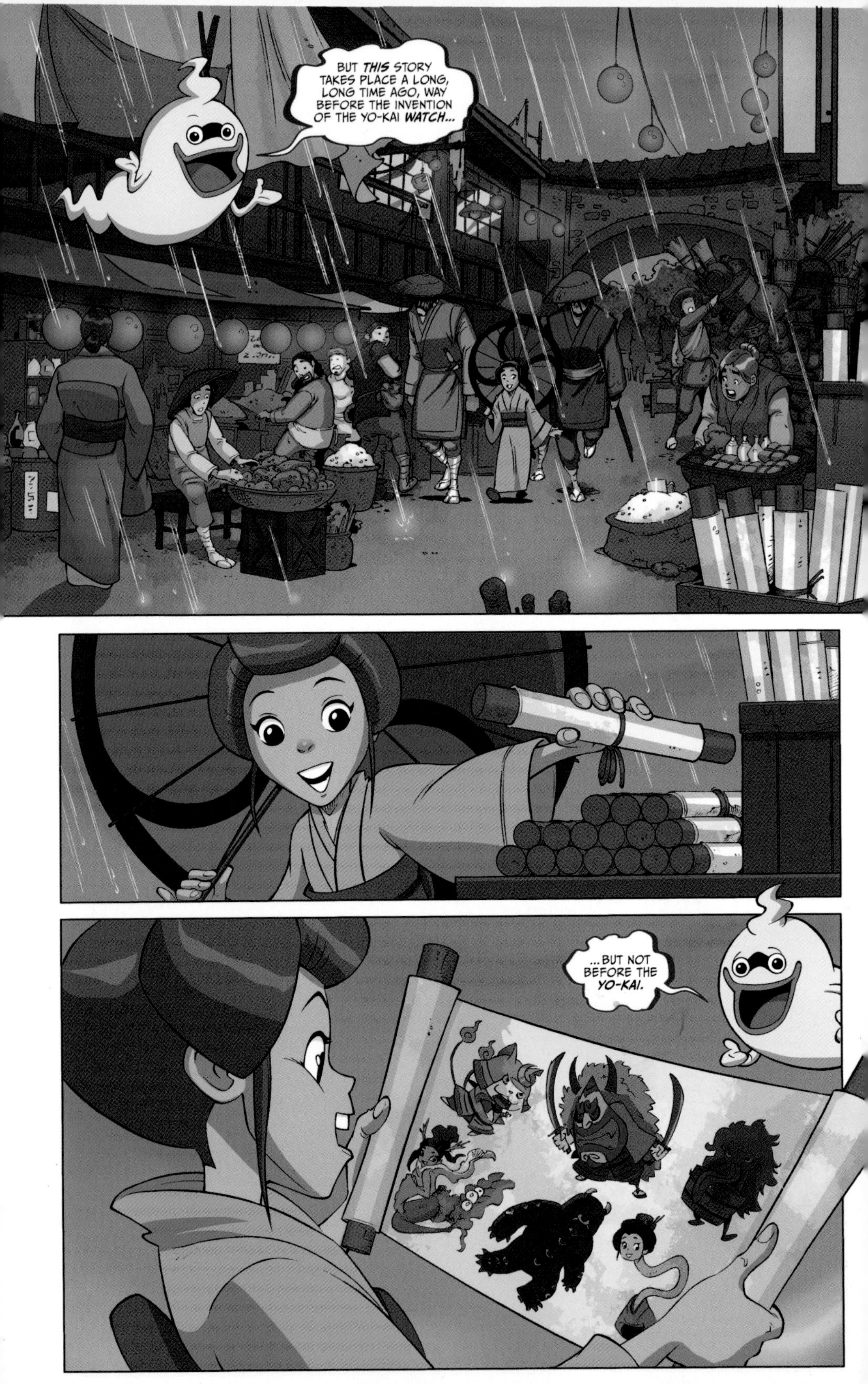
BUT THIS STORY TAKES PLACE A LONG, LONG TIME AGO, WAY BEFORE THE INVENTION OF THE YO-KAI WATCH...
...BUT NOT BEFORE THE YO-KAI.

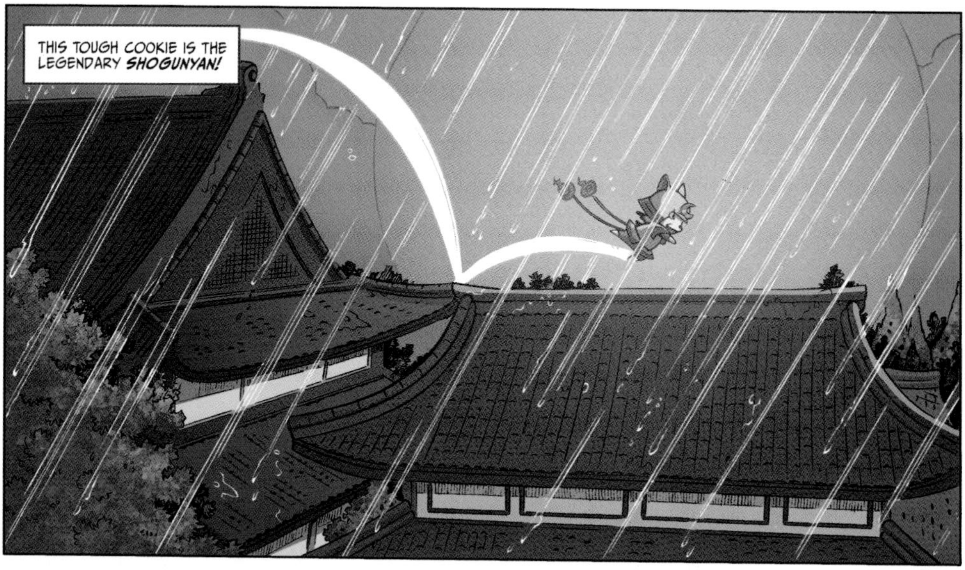
THIS TOUGH COOKIE IS THE LEGENDARY SHOGUNYAN!

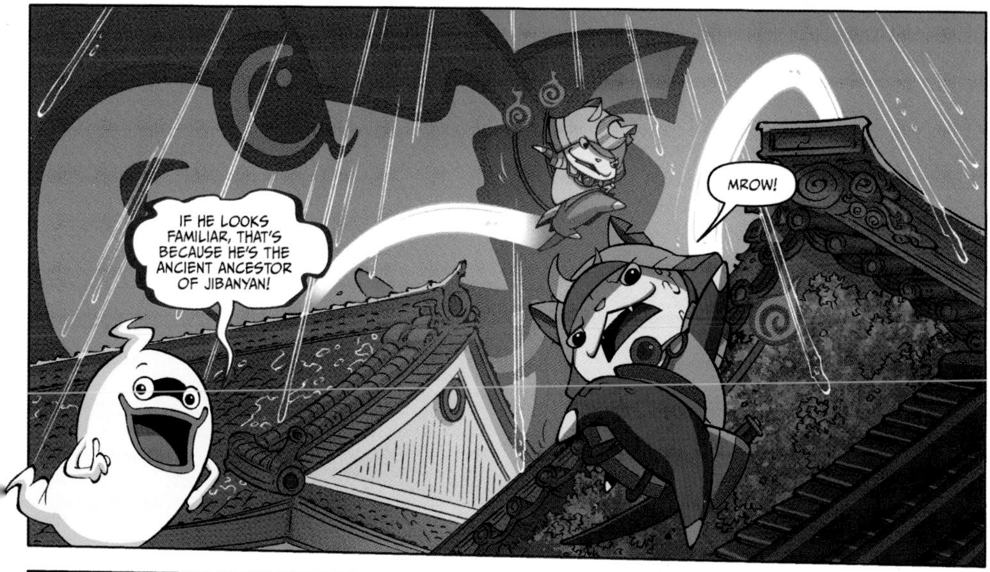
IF HE LOOKS FAMILIAR, THAT'S BECAUSE HE'S THE ANCIENT ANCESTOR OF JIBANYAN!
MROW!

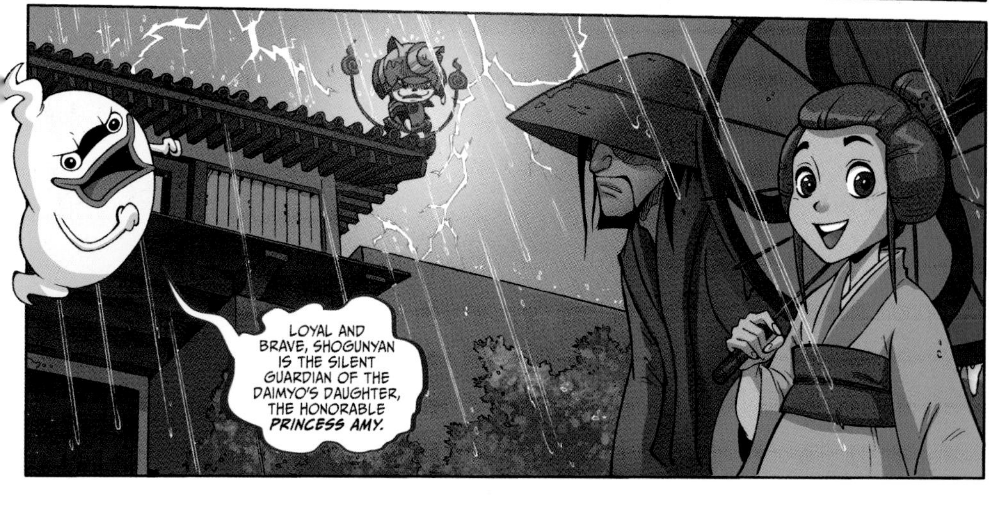
LOYAL AND BRAVE, SHOGUNYAN IS THE SILENT GUARDIAN OF THE DAIMYO'S DAUGHTER, THE HONORABLE PRINCESS AMY.

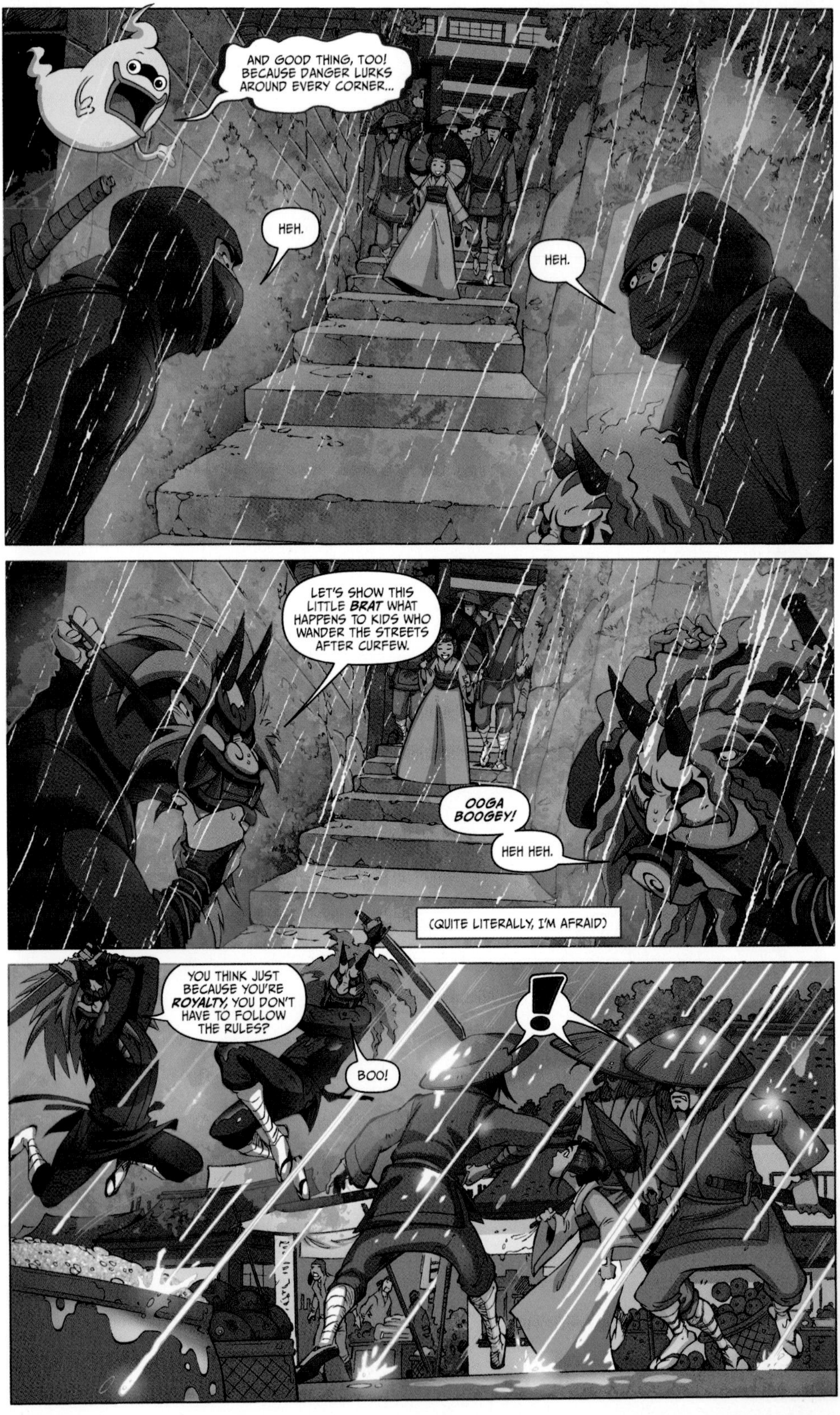
AND GOOD THING, TOO! BECAUSE DANGER LURKS AROUND EVERY CORNER...
HEH.
HEH.
LET'S SHOW THIS LITTLE BRAT WHAT HAPPENS TO KIDS WHO WANDER THE STREETS AFTER CURFEW.
OOGA BOOGEY!
HEH HEH.
(QUITE LITERALLY, I'M AFRAID)
YOU THINK JUST BECAUSE YOU'RE ROYALTY, YOU DON'T HAVE TO FOLLOW THE RULES?
!
BOO!

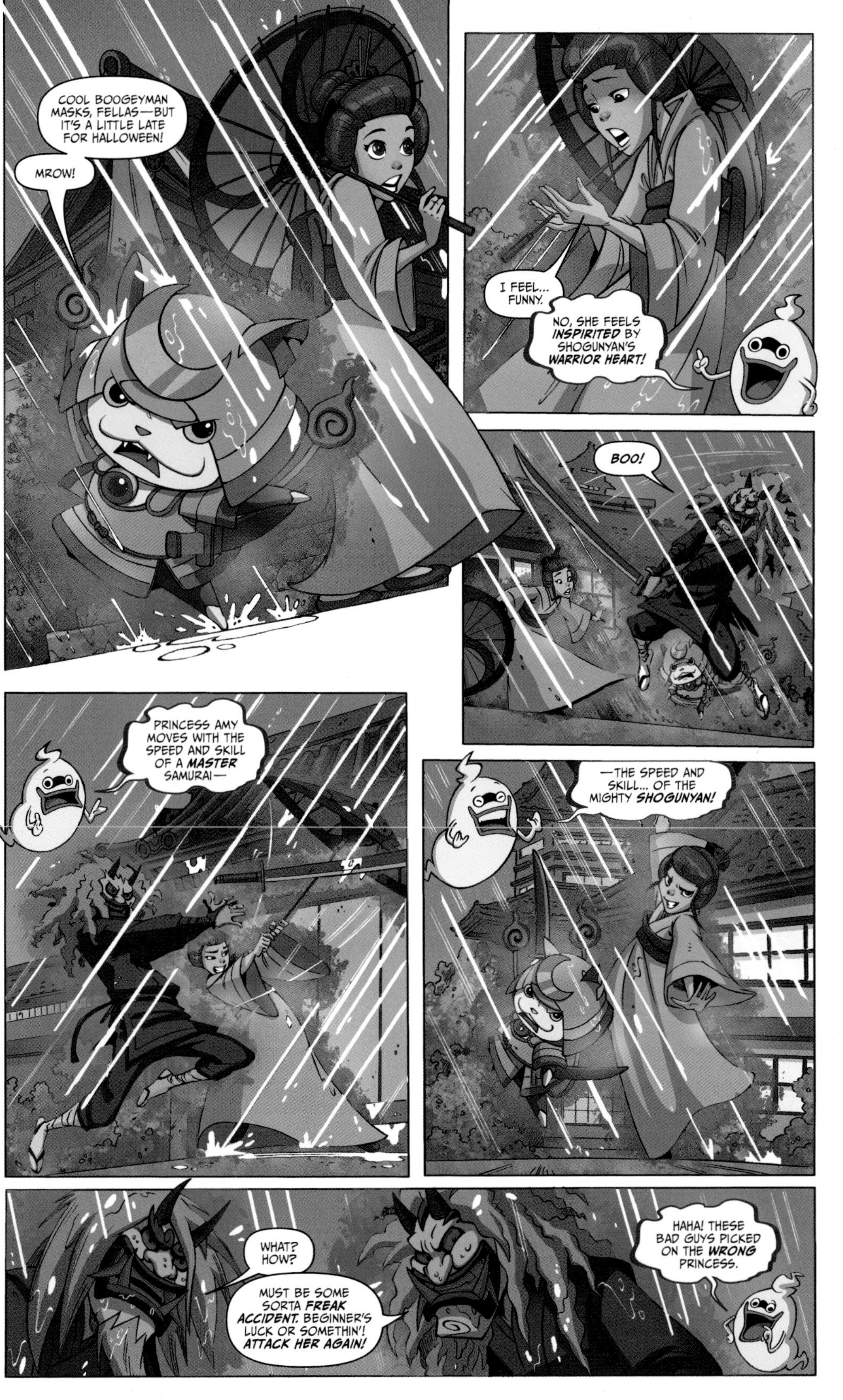

COOL BOOGEYMAN MASKS, FELLAS—BUT IT'S A LITTLE LATE FOR HALLOWEEN!
MROW!
I FEEL... FUNNY.
NO, SHE FEELS **INSPIRITED** BY SHOGUNYAN'S **WARRIOR HEART!**
BOO!
PRINCESS AMY MOVES WITH THE SPEED AND SKILL OF A **MASTER** SAMURAI—
—THE SPEED AND SKILL... OF THE MIGHTY **SHOGUNYAN!**
WHAT? HOW?
MUST BE SOME SORTA **FREAK ACCIDENT.** BEGINNER'S LUCK OR SOMETHIN'! **ATTACK HER AGAIN!**
HAHA! THESE BAD GUYS PICKED ON THE **WRONG** PRINCESS.

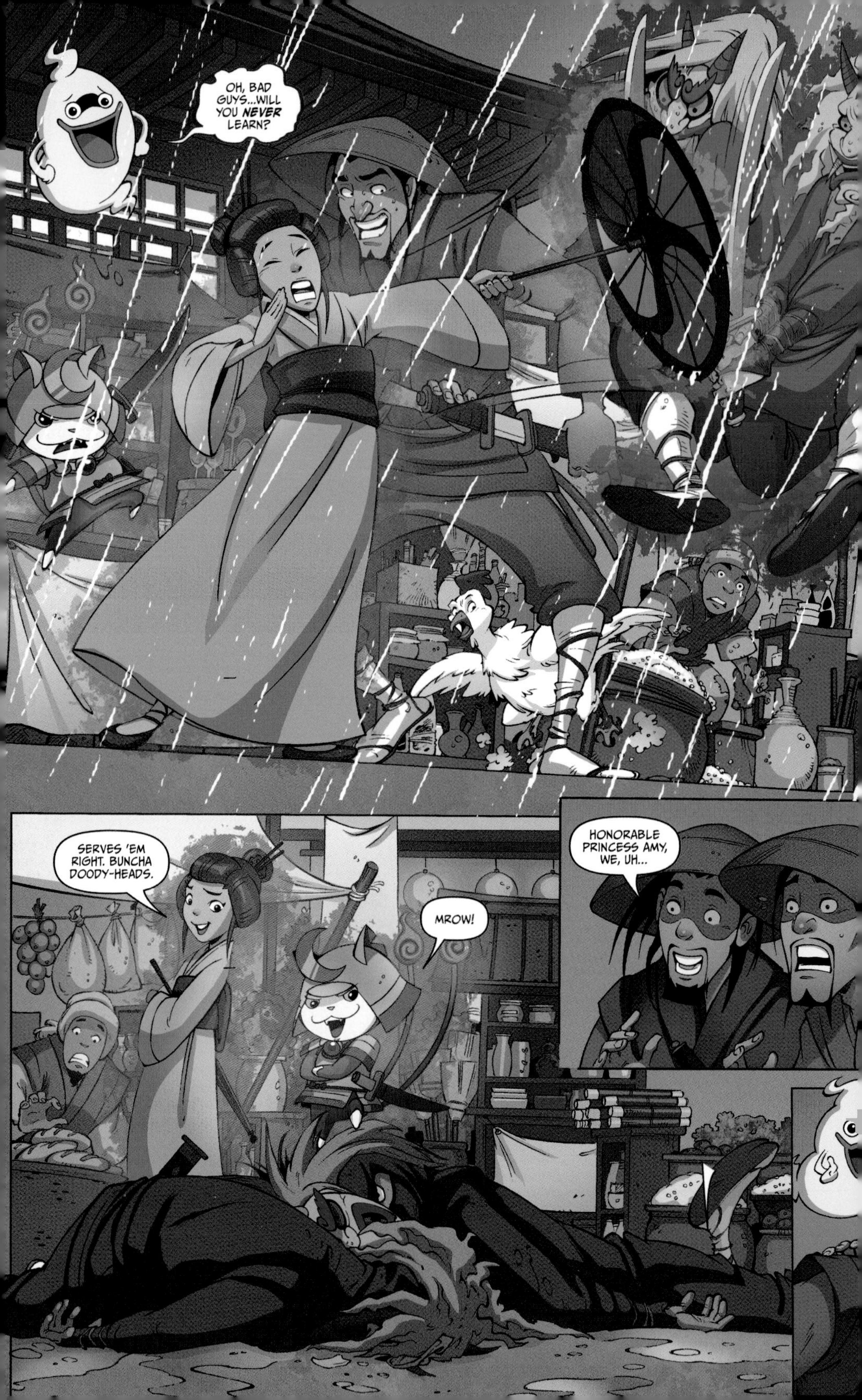
OH, BAD GUYS...WILL YOU NEVER LEARN?
SERVES 'EM RIGHT. BUNCHA DOODY-HEADS.
MROW!
HONORABLE PRINCESS AMY, WE, UH...

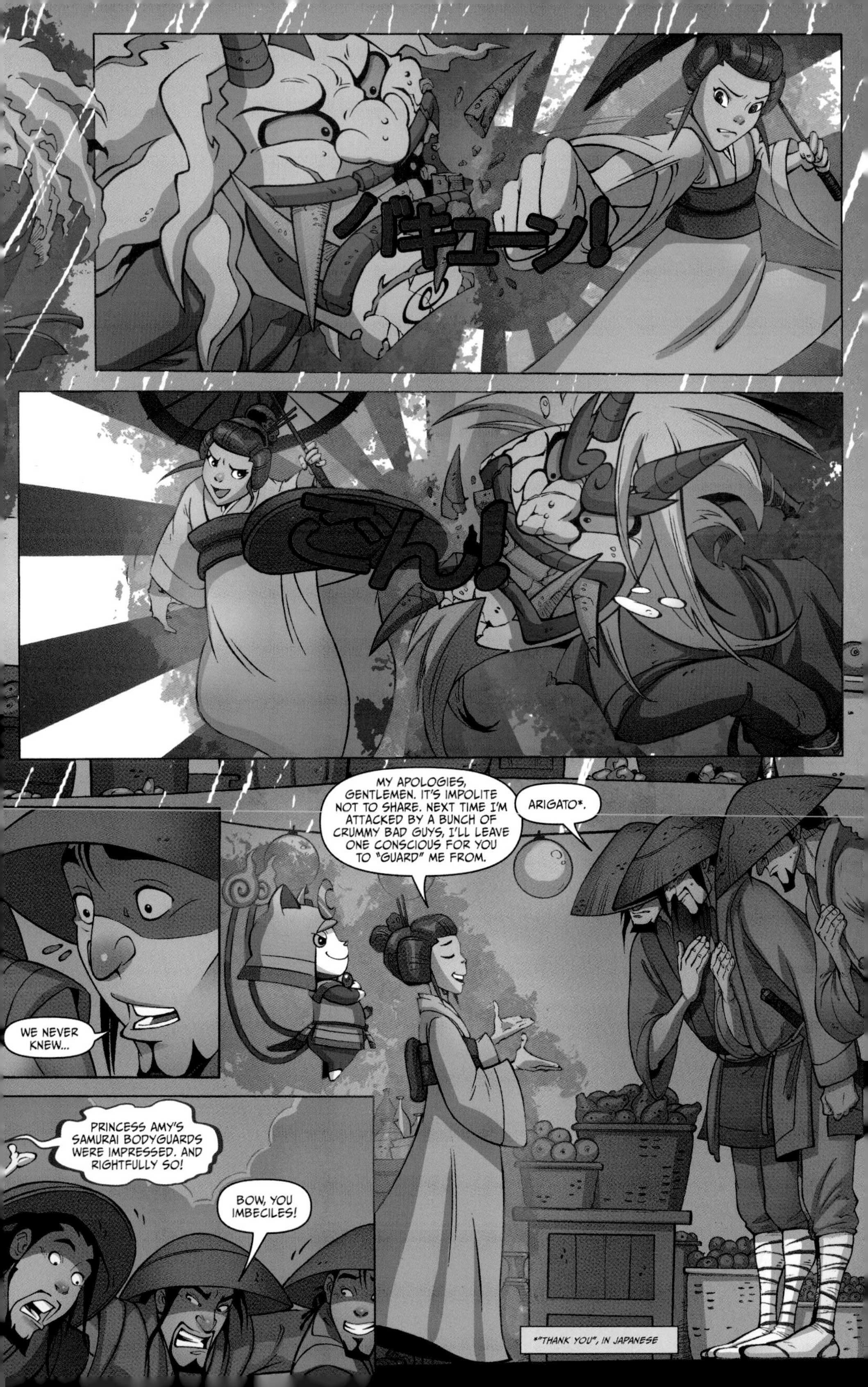
ドキューン!
ごん!
MY APOLOGIES, GENTLEMEN. IT'S IMPOLITE NOT TO SHARE. NEXT TIME I'M ATTACKED BY A BUNCH OF CRUMMY BAD GUYS, I'LL LEAVE ONE CONSCIOUS FOR YOU TO "GUARD" ME FROM.
ARIGATO*.
WE NEVER KNEW...
PRINCESS AMY'S SAMURAI BODYGUARDS WERE IMPRESSED. AND RIGHTFULLY SO!
BOW, YOU IMBECILES!
*"THANK YOU", IN JAPANESE

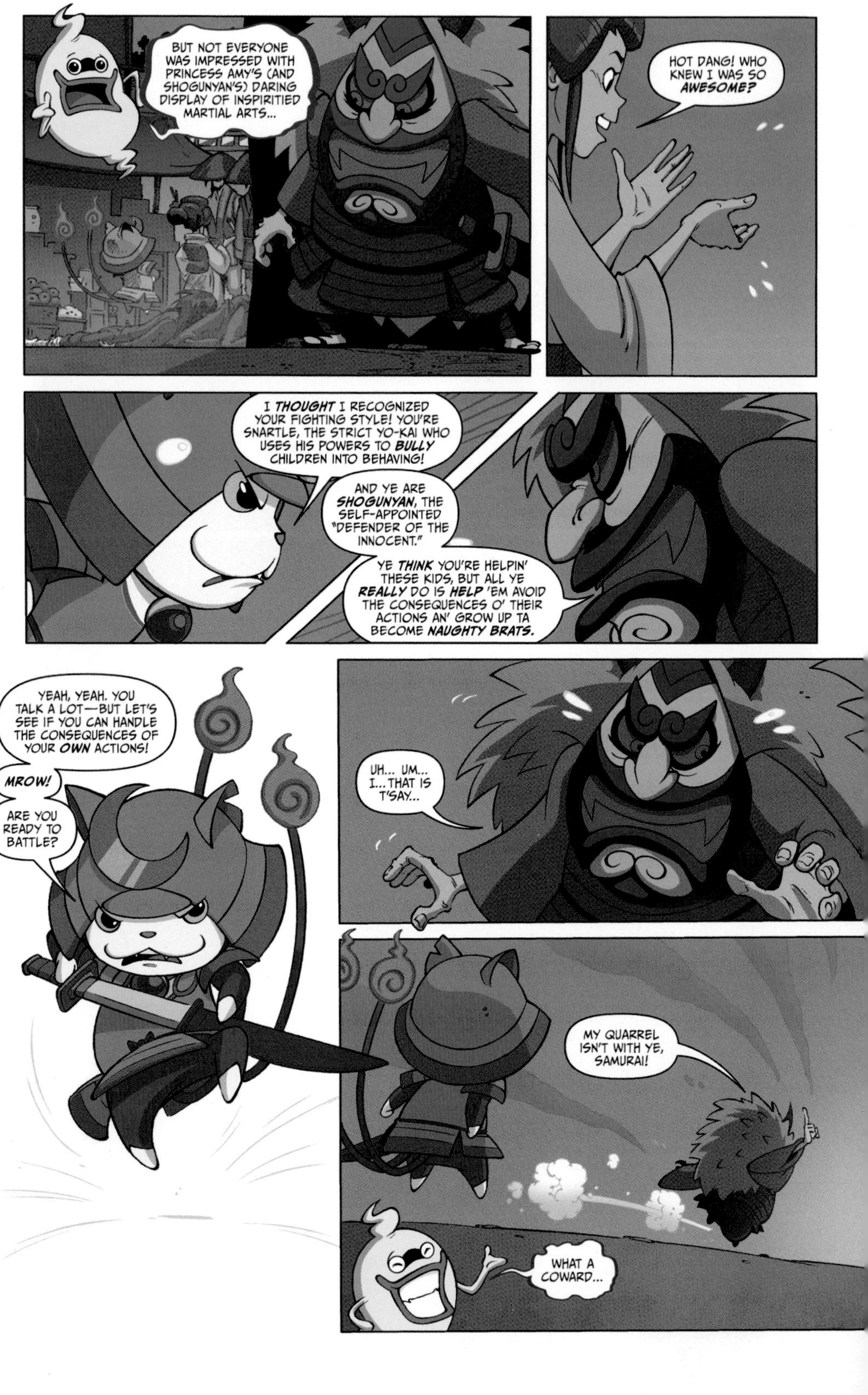
BUT NOT EVERYONE WAS IMPRESSED WITH PRINCESS AMY'S (AND SHOGUNYAN'S) DARING DISPLAY OF INSPIRITIED MARTIAL ARTS...
HOT DANG! WHO KNEW I WAS SO AWESOME?
I THOUGHT I RECOGNIZED YOUR FIGHTING STYLE! YOU'RE SNARTLE, THE STRICT YO-KAI WHO USES HIS POWERS TO BULLY CHILDREN INTO BEHAVING!
AND YE ARE SHOGUNYAN, THE SELF-APPOINTED "DEFENDER OF THE INNOCENT."
YE THINK YOU'RE HELPIN' THESE KIDS, BUT ALL YE REALLY DO IS HELP 'EM AVOID THE CONSEQUENCES O' THEIR ACTIONS AN' GROW UP TA BECOME NAUGHTY BRATS.
YEAH, YEAH. YOU TALK A LOT—BUT LET'S SEE IF YOU CAN HANDLE THE CONSEQUENCES OF YOUR OWN ACTIONS!
MROW!
ARE YOU READY TO BATTLE?
UH... UM... I... THAT IS T'SAY...
MY QUARREL ISN'T WITH YE, SAMURAI!
WHAT A COWARD...

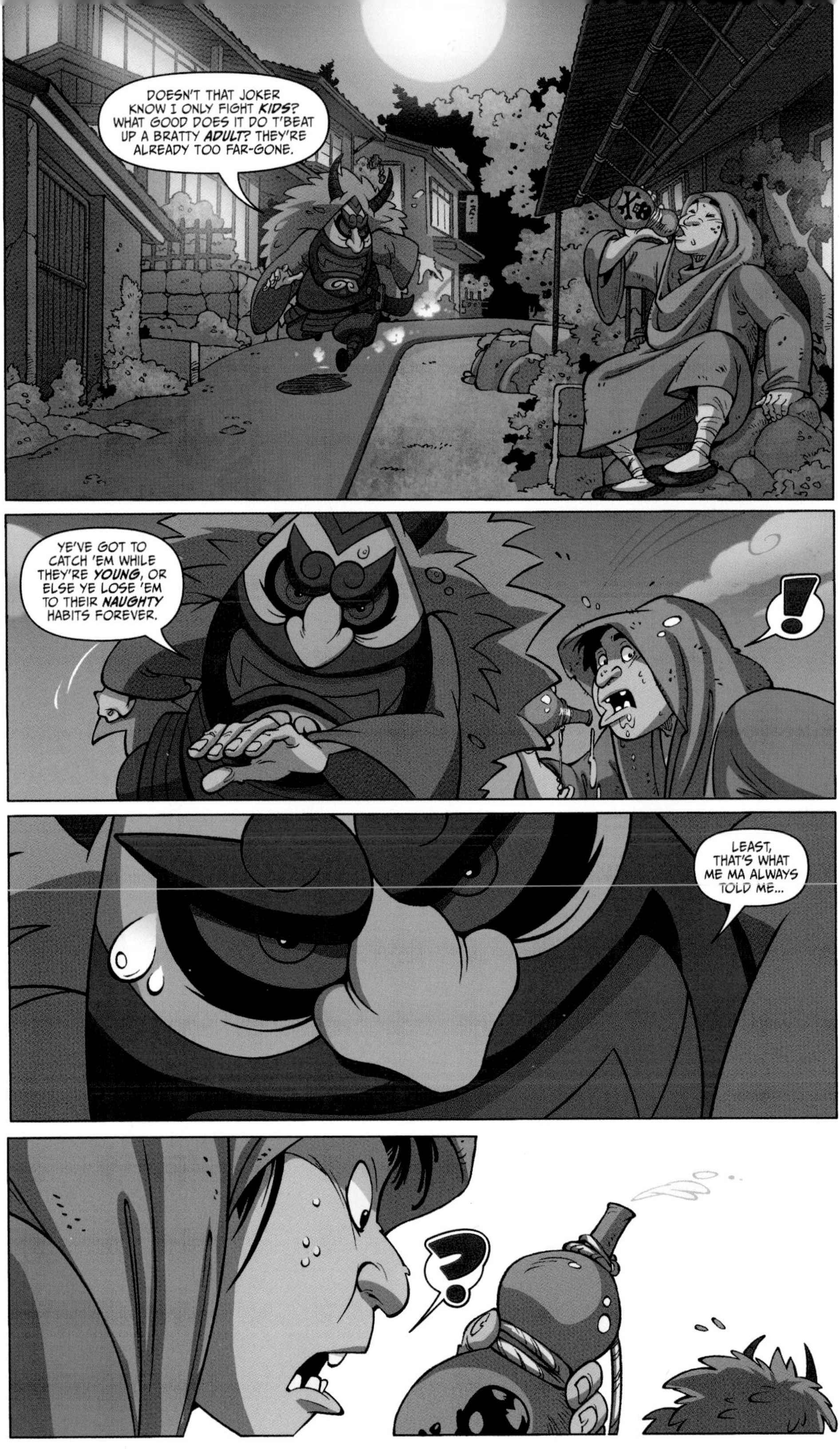
DOESN'T THAT JOKER KNOW I ONLY FIGHT KIDS? WHAT GOOD DOES IT DO T'BEAT UP A BRATTY ADULT? THEY'RE ALREADY TOO FAR-GONE.
YE'VE GOT TO CATCH 'EM WHILE THEY'RE YOUNG, OR ELSE YE LOSE 'EM TO THEIR NAUGHTY HABITS FOREVER.
!
LEAST, THAT'S WHAT ME MA ALWAYS TOLD ME...
?

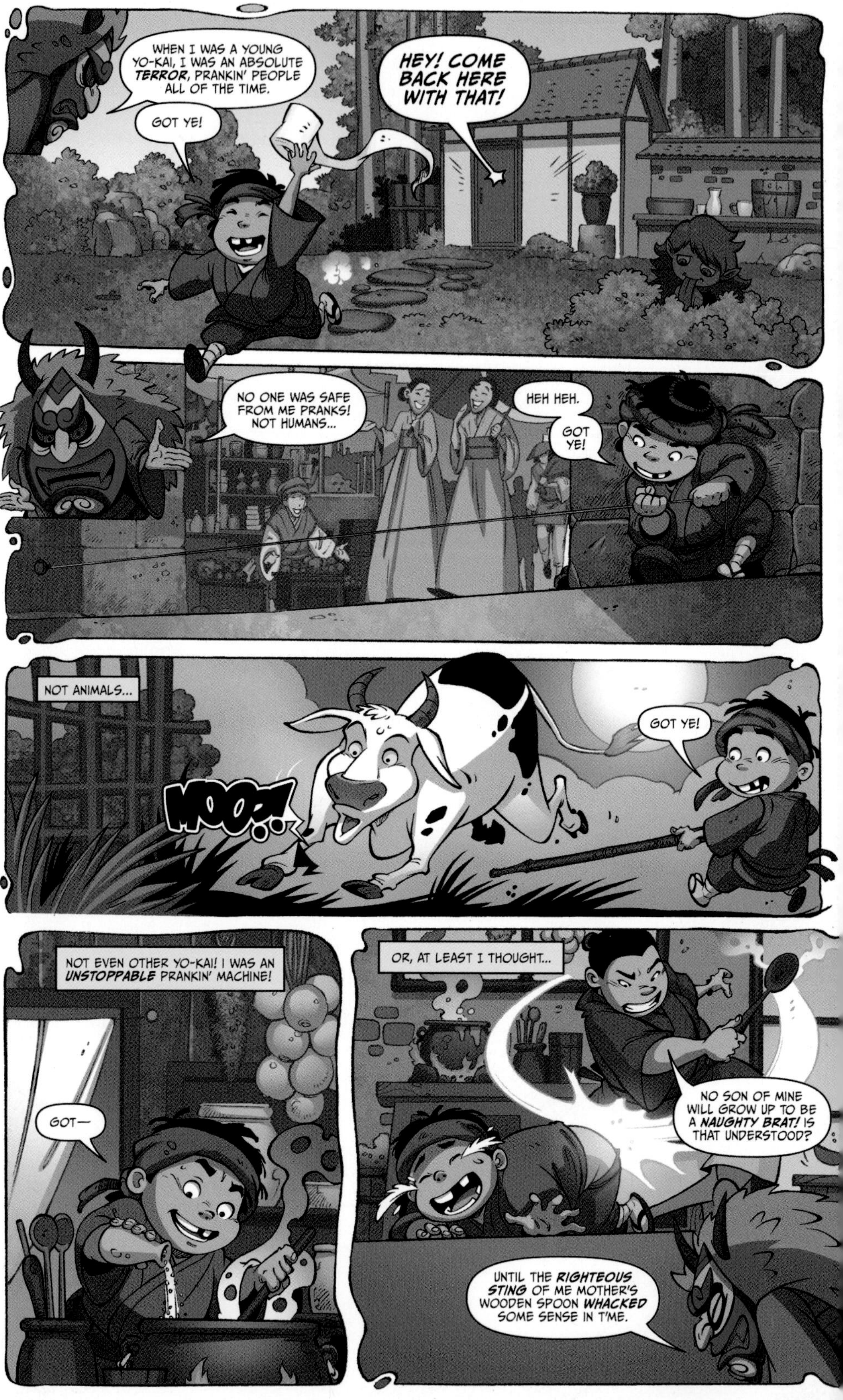
WHEN I WAS A YOUNG YO-KAI, I WAS AN ABSOLUTE *TERROR*, PRANKIN' PEOPLE ALL OF THE TIME.
GOT YE!
HEY! COME BACK HERE WITH THAT!
NO ONE WAS SAFE FROM ME PRANKS! NOT HUMANS...
HEH HEH.
GOT YE!
NOT ANIMALS...
GOT YE!
MOO?!
NOT EVEN OTHER YO-KAI! I WAS AN *UNSTOPPABLE* PRANKIN' MACHINE!
GOT—
OR, AT LEAST I THOUGHT...
NO SON OF MINE WILL GROW UP TO BE A *NAUGHTY BRAT!* IS THAT UNDERSTOOD?
UNTIL THE *RIGHTEOUS STING* OF ME MOTHER'S WOODEN SPOON *WHACKED* SOME SENSE IN T'ME.

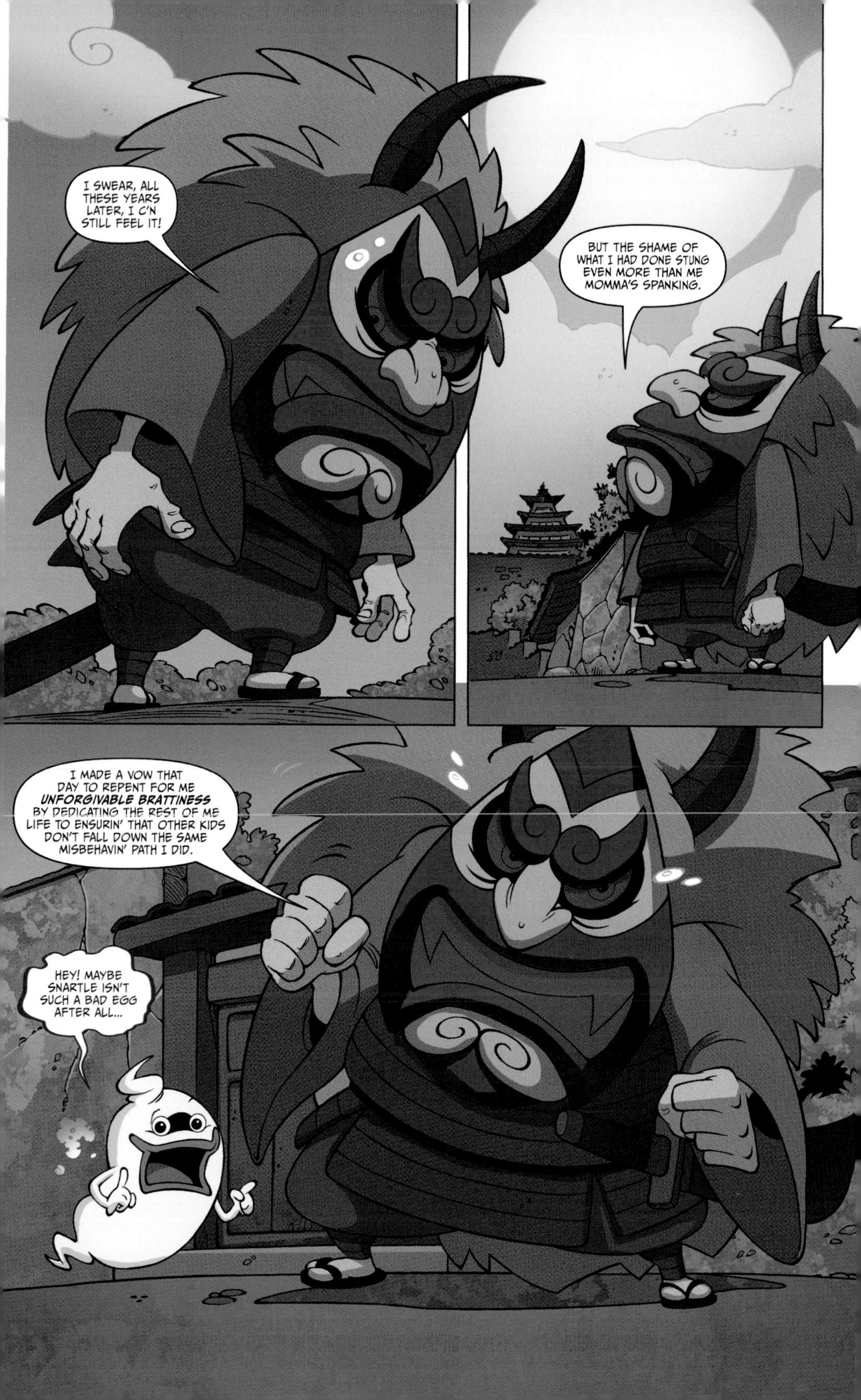
I SWEAR, ALL THESE YEARS LATER, I C'N STILL FEEL IT!
BUT THE SHAME OF WHAT I HAD DONE STUNG EVEN MORE THAN ME MOMMA'S SPANKING.
I MADE A VOW THAT DAY TO REPENT FOR ME *UNFORGIVABLE BRATTINESS* BY DEDICATING THE REST OF ME LIFE TO ENSURIN' THAT OTHER KIDS DON'T FALL DOWN THE SAME MISBEHAVIN' PATH I DID.
HEY! MAYBE SNARTLE ISN'T SUCH A BAD EGG AFTER ALL...

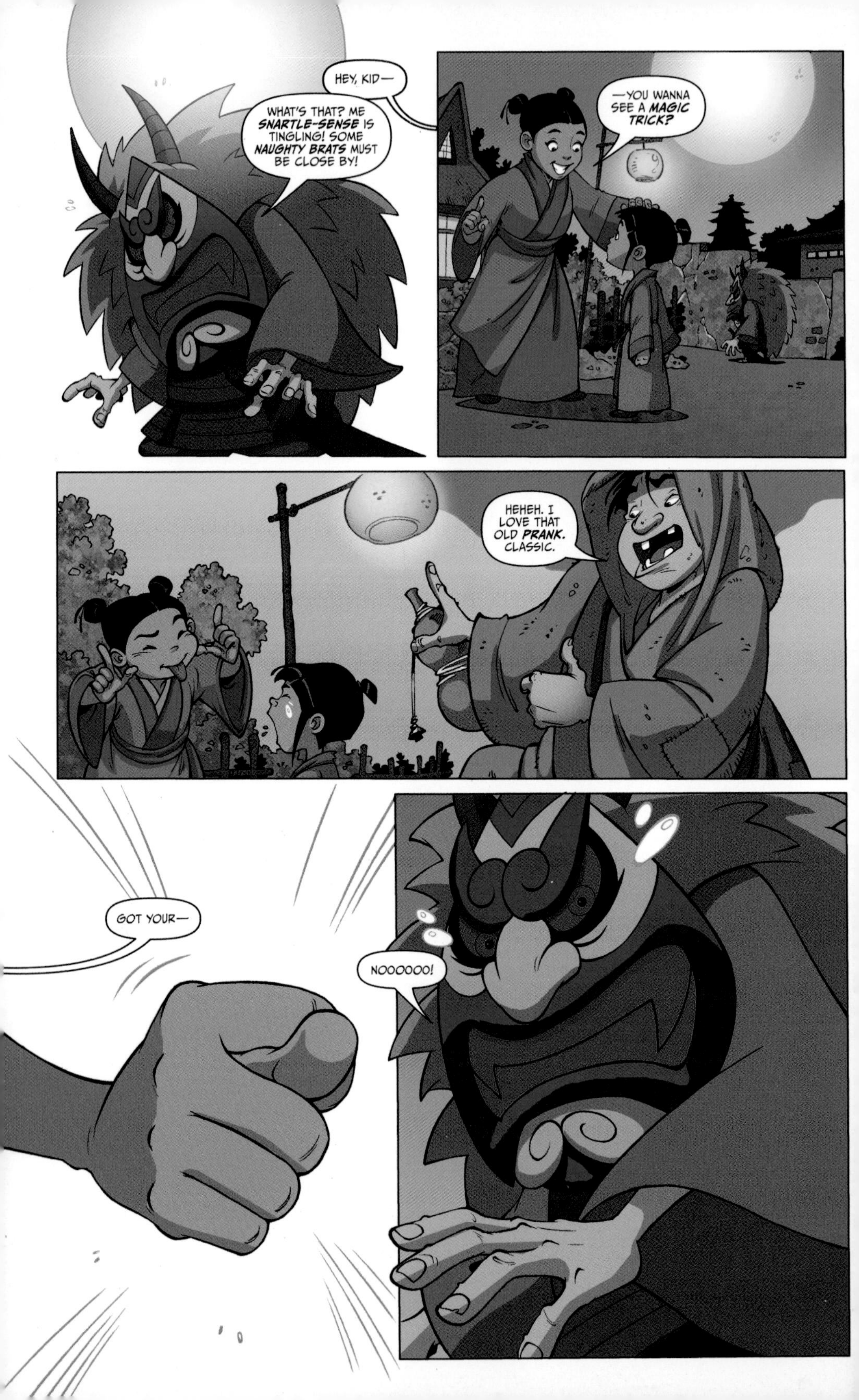
HEY, KID—
WHAT'S THAT? ME SNARTLE-SENSE IS TINGLING! SOME NAUGHTY BRATS MUST BE CLOSE BY!
—YOU WANNA SEE A MAGIC TRICK?
HEHEH. I LOVE THAT OLD PRANK. CLASSIC.
GOT YOUR—
NOOOOOO!

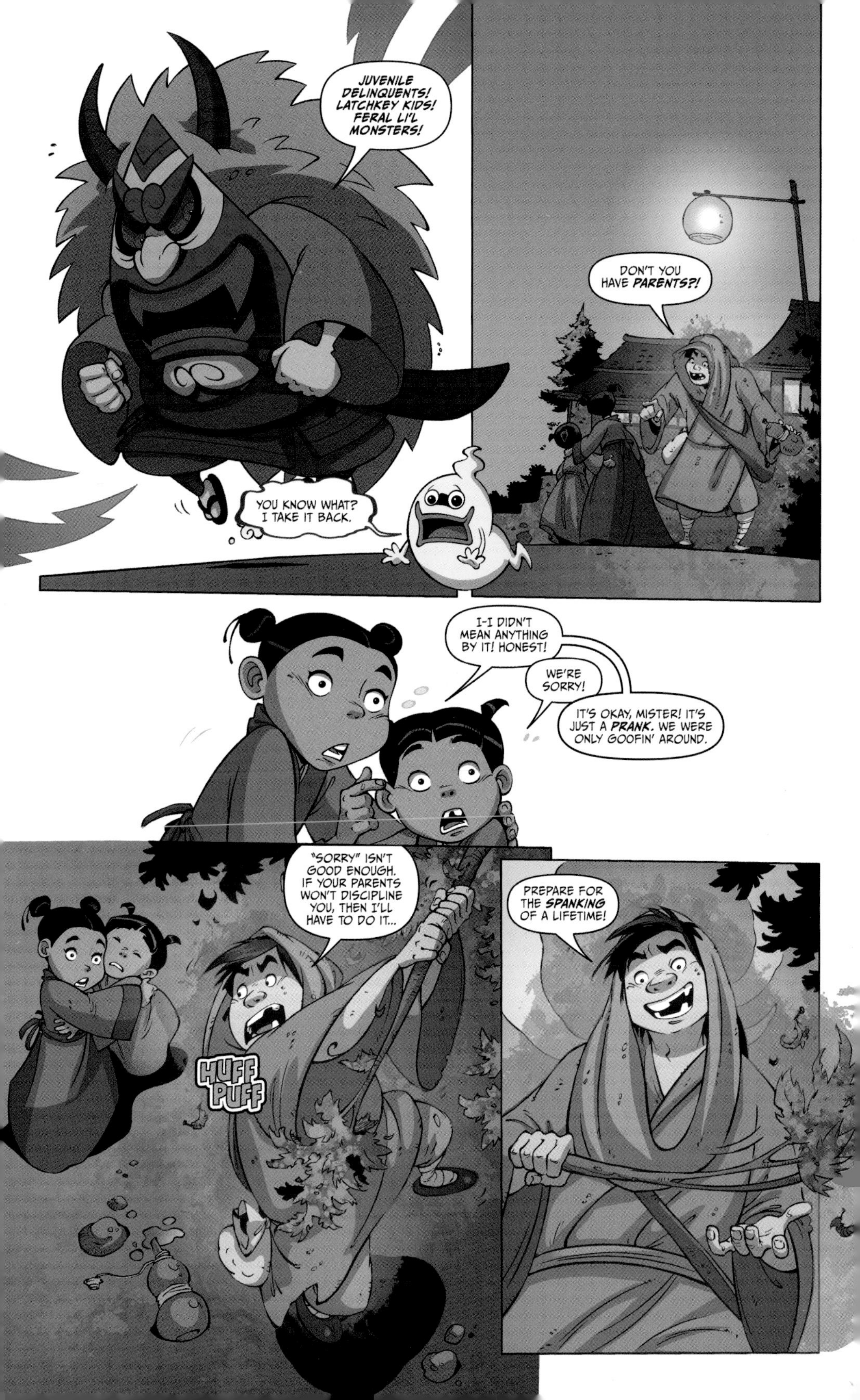
JUVENILE DELINQUENTS! LATCHKEY KIDS! FERAL LI'L MONSTERS!
YOU KNOW WHAT? I TAKE IT BACK.
DON'T YOU HAVE PARENTS?!
I-I DIDN'T MEAN ANYTHING BY IT! HONEST!
WE'RE SORRY!
IT'S OKAY, MISTER! IT'S JUST A PRANK. WE WERE ONLY GOOFIN' AROUND.
"SORRY" ISN'T GOOD ENOUGH. IF YOUR PARENTS WON'T DISCIPLINE YOU, THEN I'LL HAVE TO DO IT...
HUFF PUFF
PREPARE FOR THE SPANKING OF A LIFETIME!

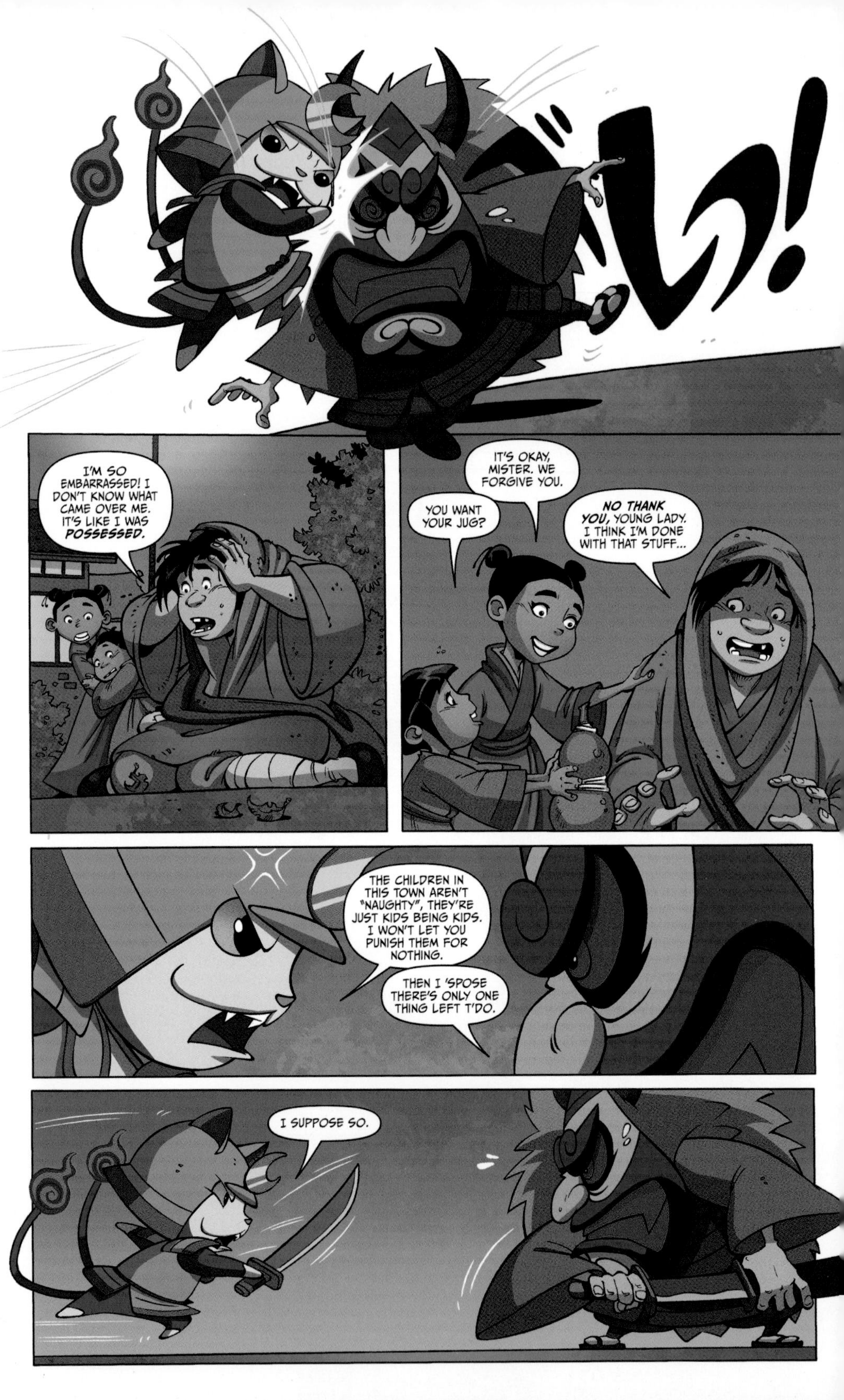
I'M SO EMBARRASSED! I DON'T KNOW WHAT CAME OVER ME. IT'S LIKE I WAS **POSSESSED.**
YOU WANT YOUR JUG?
IT'S OKAY, MISTER. WE FORGIVE YOU.
NO THANK YOU, YOUNG LADY. I THINK I'M DONE WITH THAT STUFF...
THE CHILDREN IN THIS TOWN AREN'T "NAUGHTY", THEY'RE JUST KIDS BEING KIDS. I WON'T LET YOU PUNISH THEM FOR NOTHING.
THEN I 'SPOSE THERE'S ONLY ONE THING LEFT T'DO.
I SUPPOSE SO.

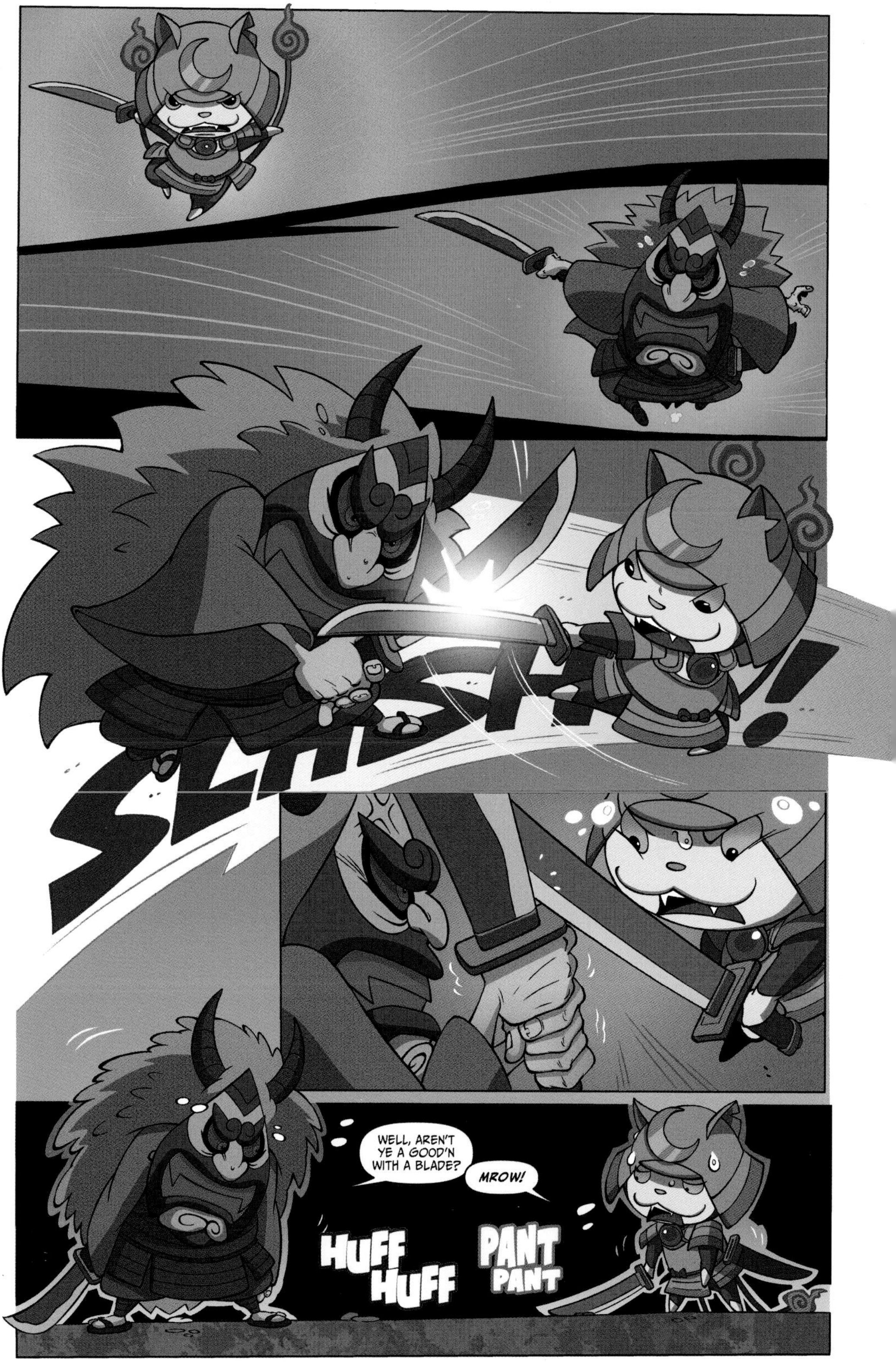
WELL, AREN'T YE A GOOD'N WITH A BLADE?
MROW!
HUFF HUFF
PANT PANT

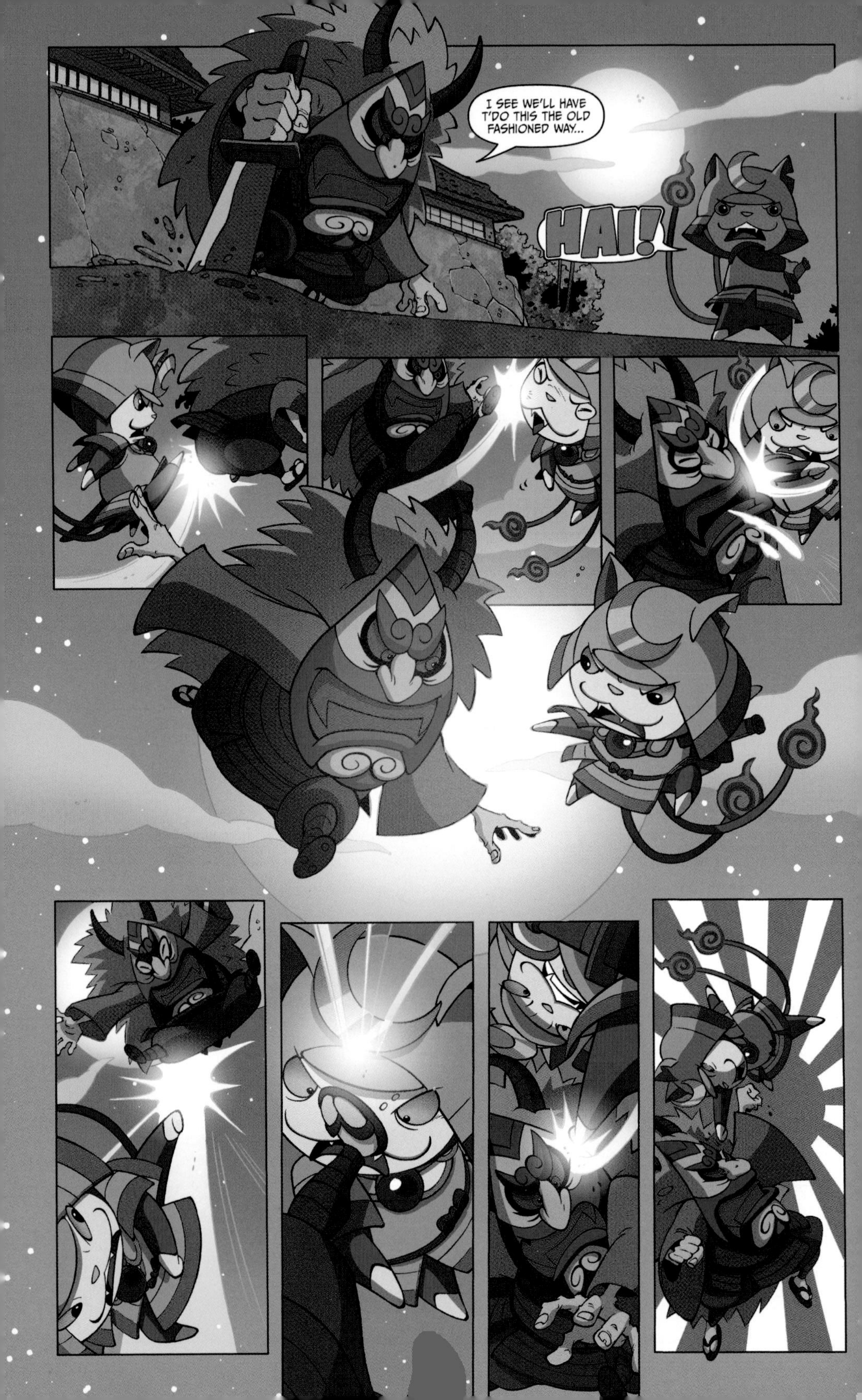
I SEE WE'LL HAVE T'DO THIS THE OLD FASHIONED WAY...
HAI!

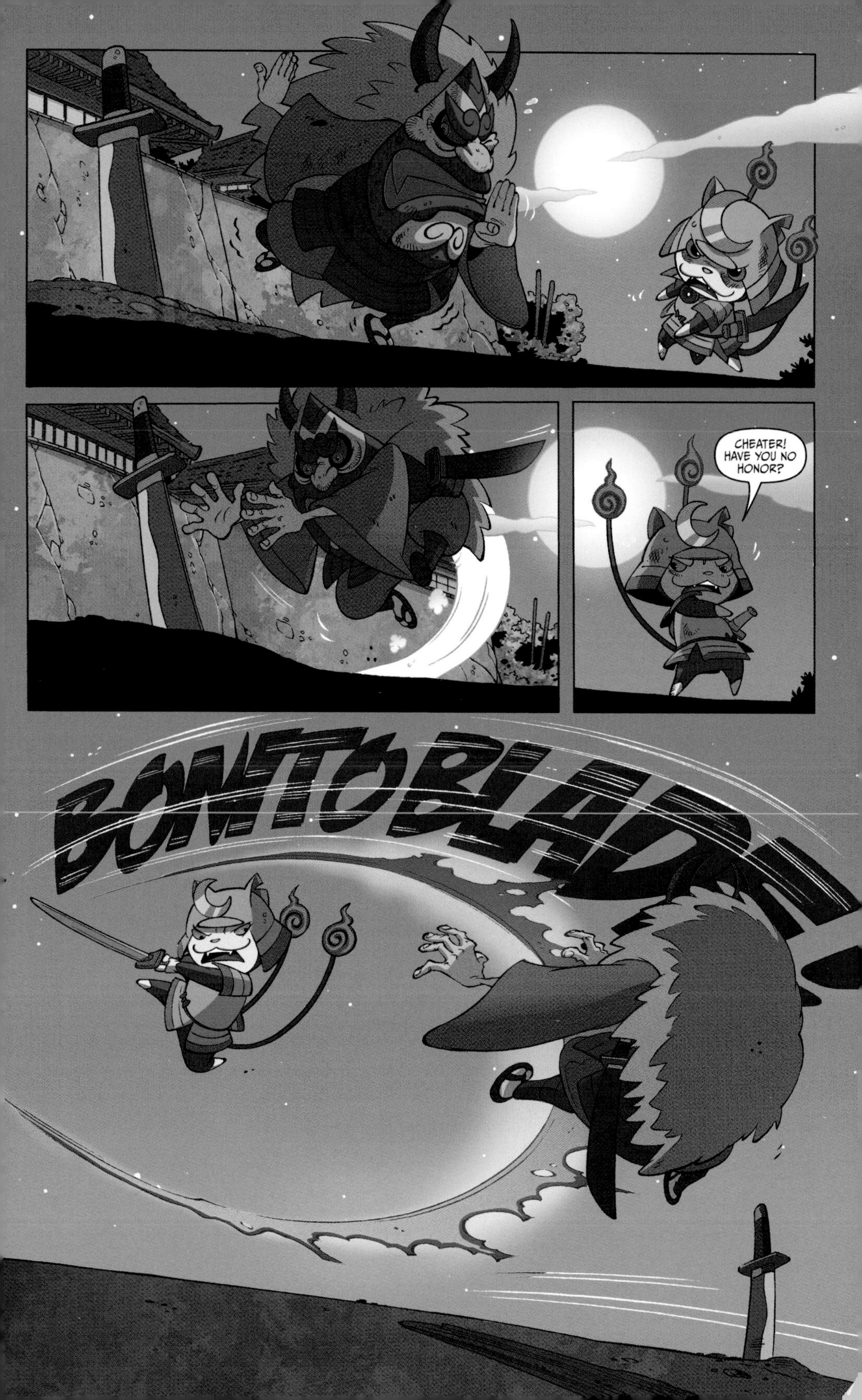
CHEATER! HAVE YOU NO HONOR?
BONITO BLADE!

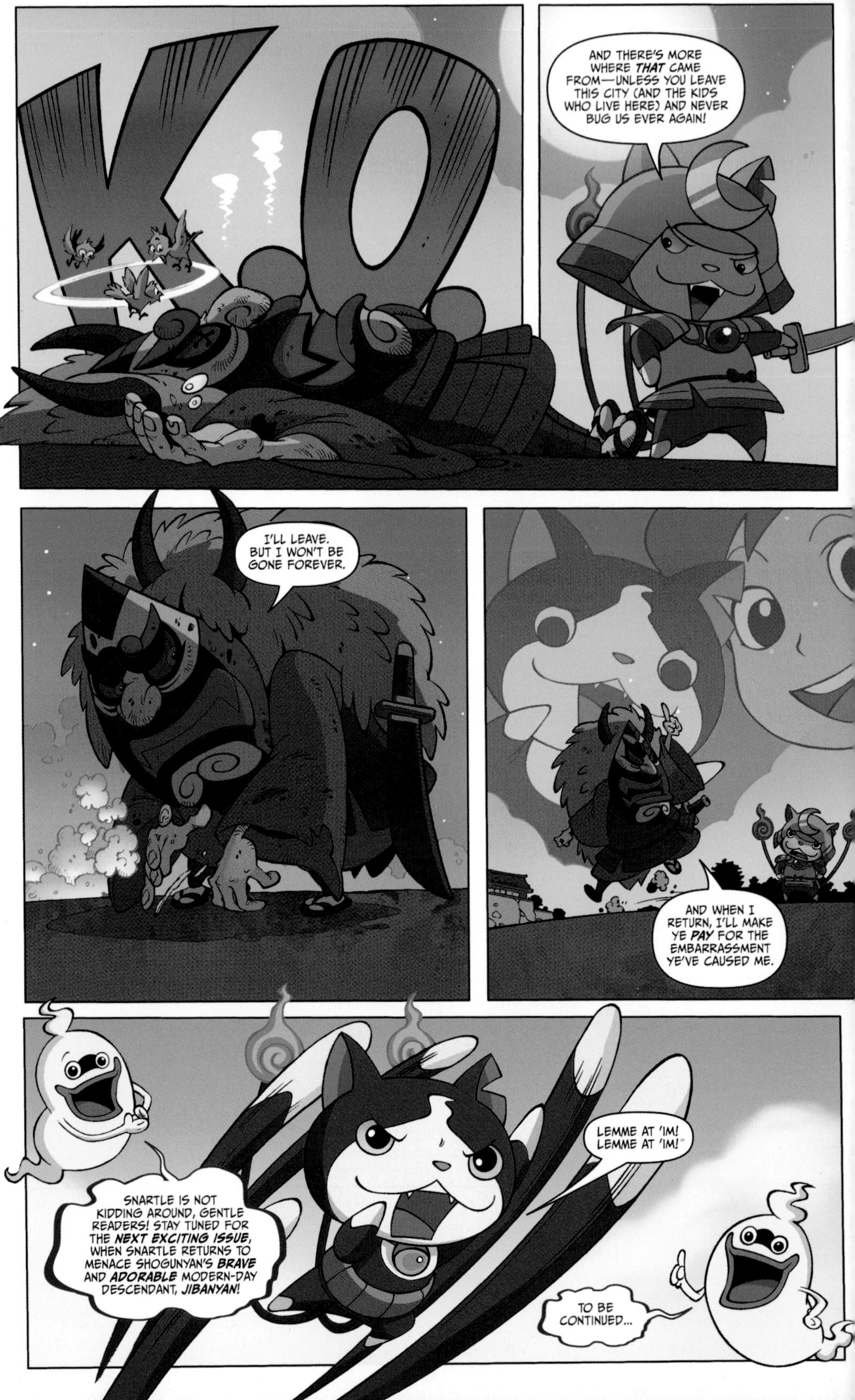
KO
AND THERE'S MORE WHERE THAT CAME FROM—UNLESS YOU LEAVE THIS CITY (AND THE KIDS WHO LIVE HERE) AND NEVER BUG US EVER AGAIN!
I'LL LEAVE. BUT I WON'T BE GONE FOREVER.
AND WHEN I RETURN, I'LL MAKE YE PAY FOR THE EMBARRASSMENT YE'VE CAUSED ME.
SNARTLE IS NOT KIDDING AROUND, GENTLE READERS! STAY TUNED FOR THE NEXT EXCITING ISSUE, WHEN SNARTLE RETURNS TO MENACE SHOGUNYAN'S BRAVE AND ADORABLE MODERN-DAY DESCENDANT, JIBANYAN!
LEMME AT 'IM! LEMME AT 'IM!
TO BE CONTINUED...

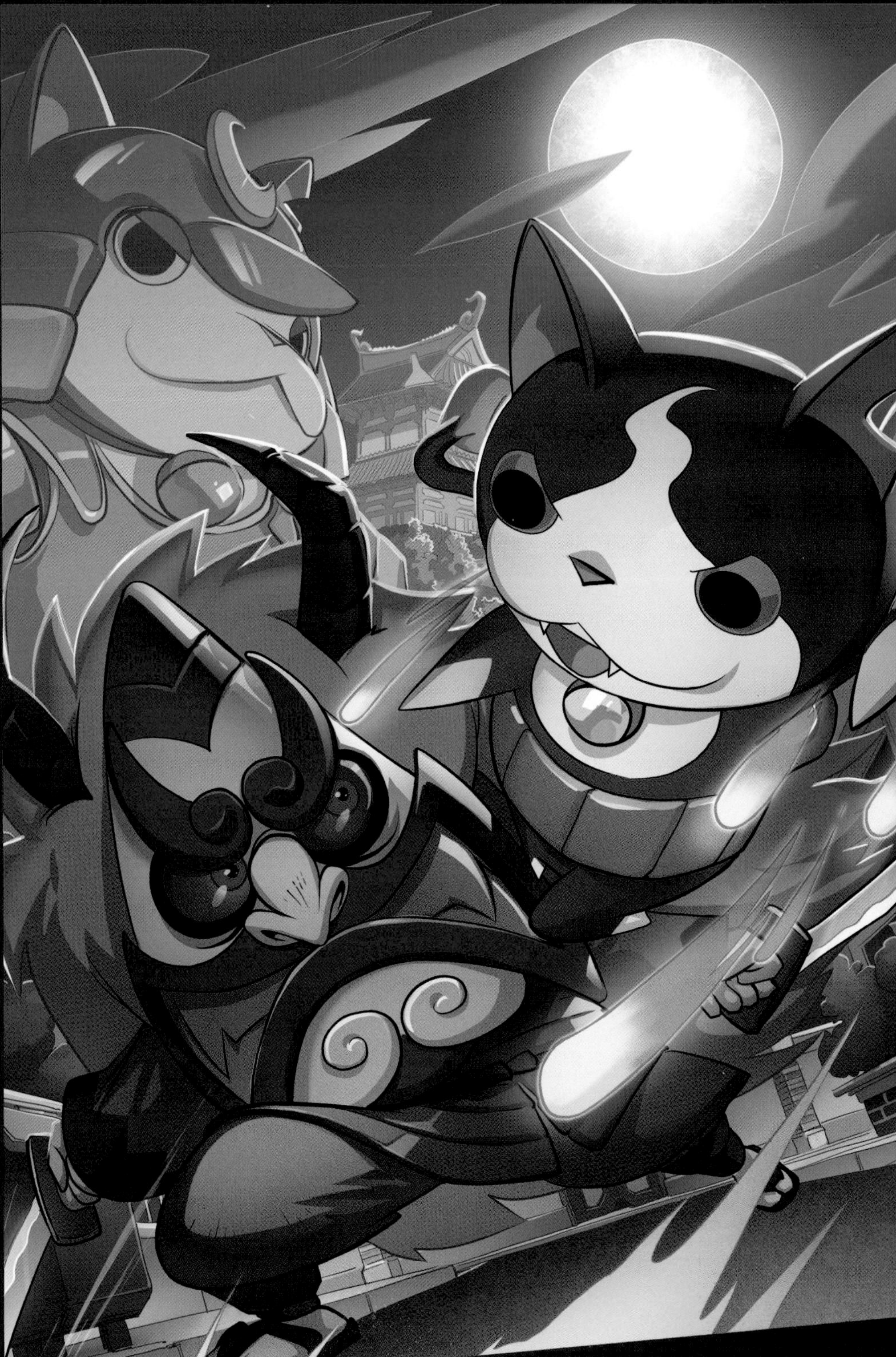

COVER ART
DONO SACHNEZ ALMARA

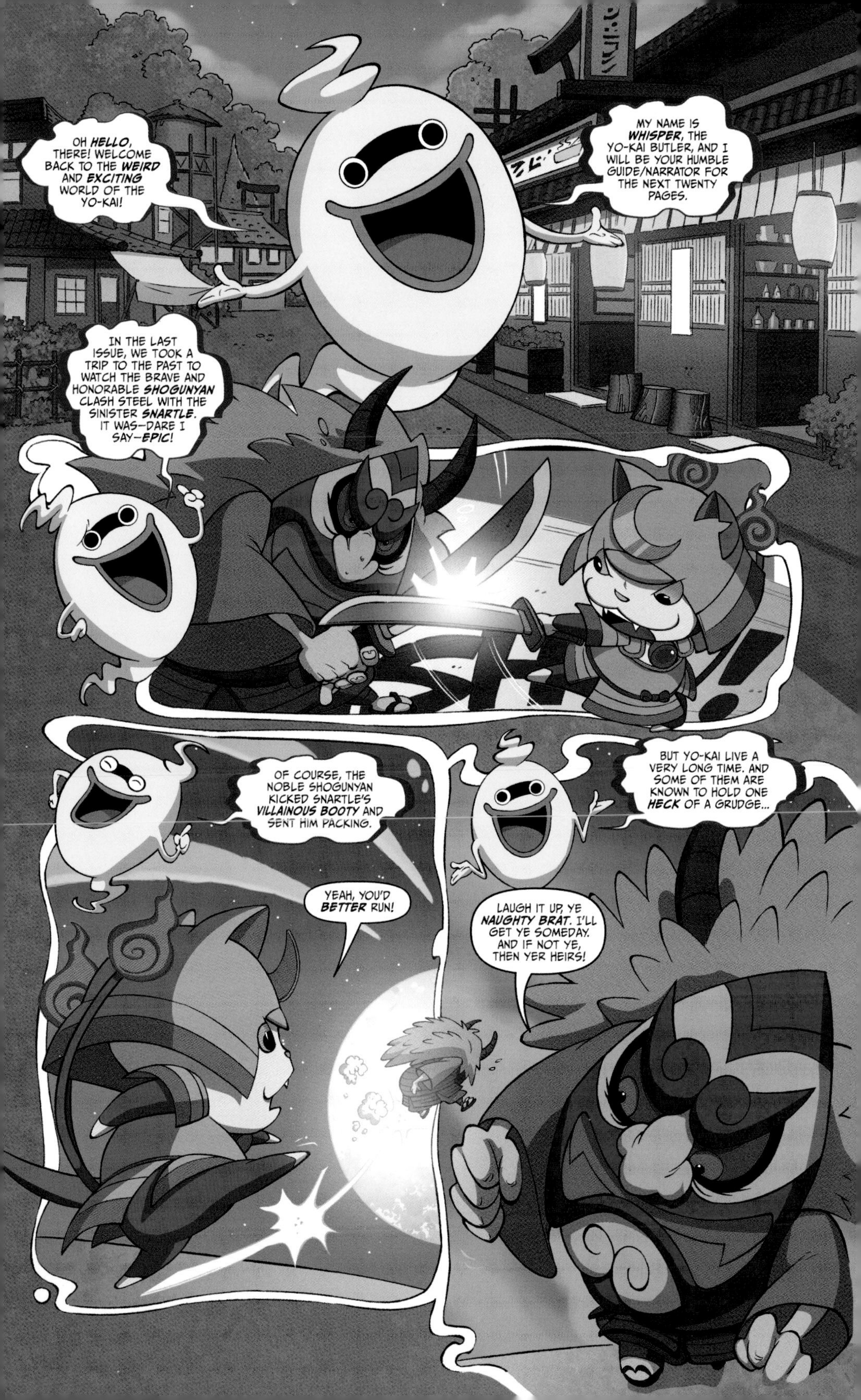
OH **HELLO**, THERE! WELCOME BACK TO THE **WEIRD** AND **EXCITING** WORLD OF THE YO-KAI!
MY NAME IS **WHISPER**, THE YO-KAI BUTLER, AND I WILL BE YOUR HUMBLE GUIDE/NARRATOR FOR THE NEXT TWENTY PAGES.
IN THE LAST ISSUE, WE TOOK A TRIP TO THE PAST TO WATCH THE BRAVE AND HONORABLE **SHOGUNYAN** CLASH STEEL WITH THE SINISTER **SNARTLE**. IT WAS—DARE I SAY—**EPIC**!
OF COURSE, THE NOBLE SHOGUNYAN KICKED SNARTLE'S **VILLAINOUS BOOTY** AND SENT HIM PACKING.
YEAH, YOU'D **BETTER** RUN!
BUT YO-KAI LIVE A VERY LONG TIME. AND SOME OF THEM ARE KNOWN TO HOLD ONE **HECK** OF A GRUDGE...
LAUGH IT UP, YE **NAUGHTY BRAT**. I'LL GET YE SOMEDAY. AND IF NOT YE, THEN YER HEIRS!

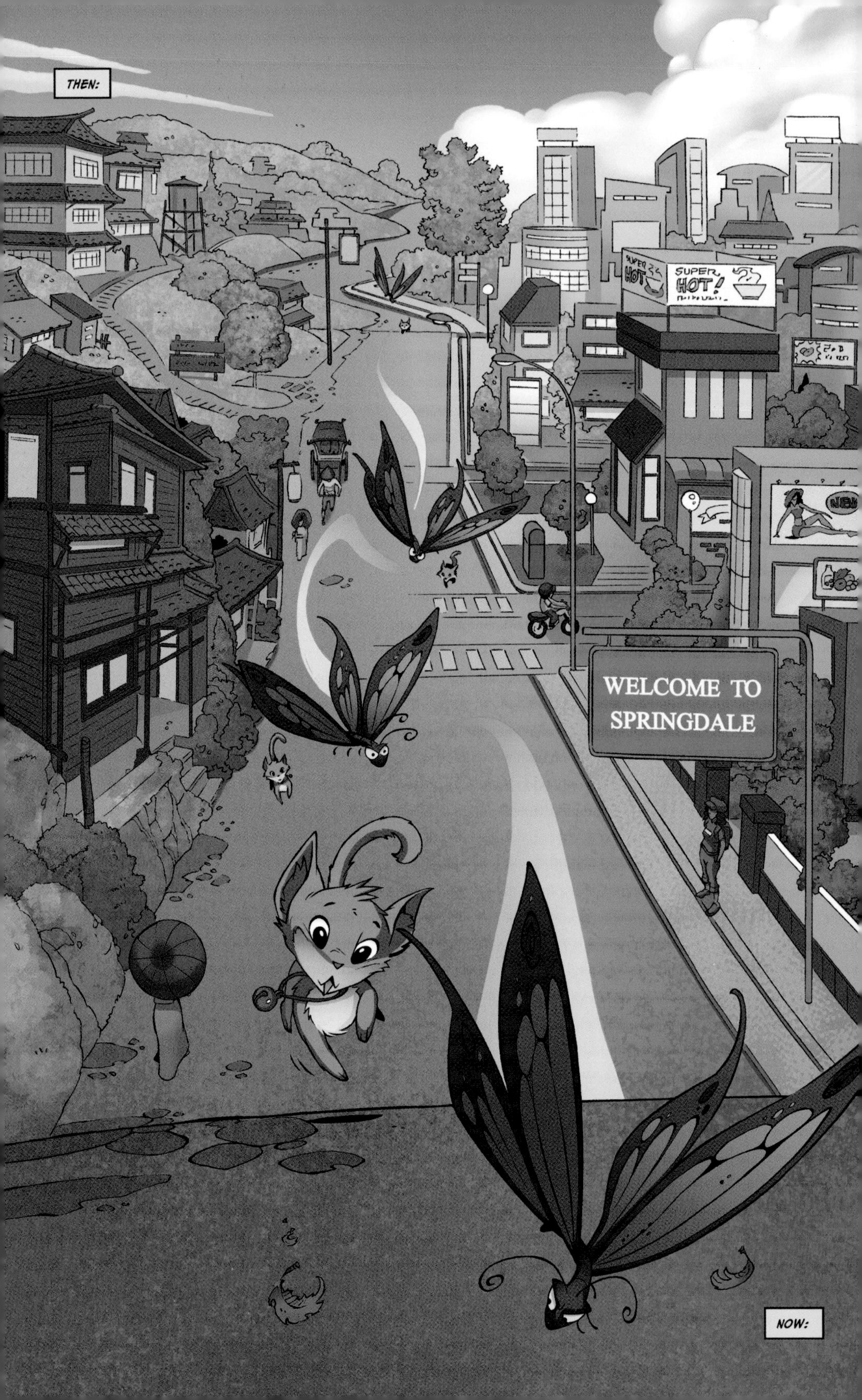
THEN:
SUPER HOT!
WELCOME TO SPRINGDALE
NOW:

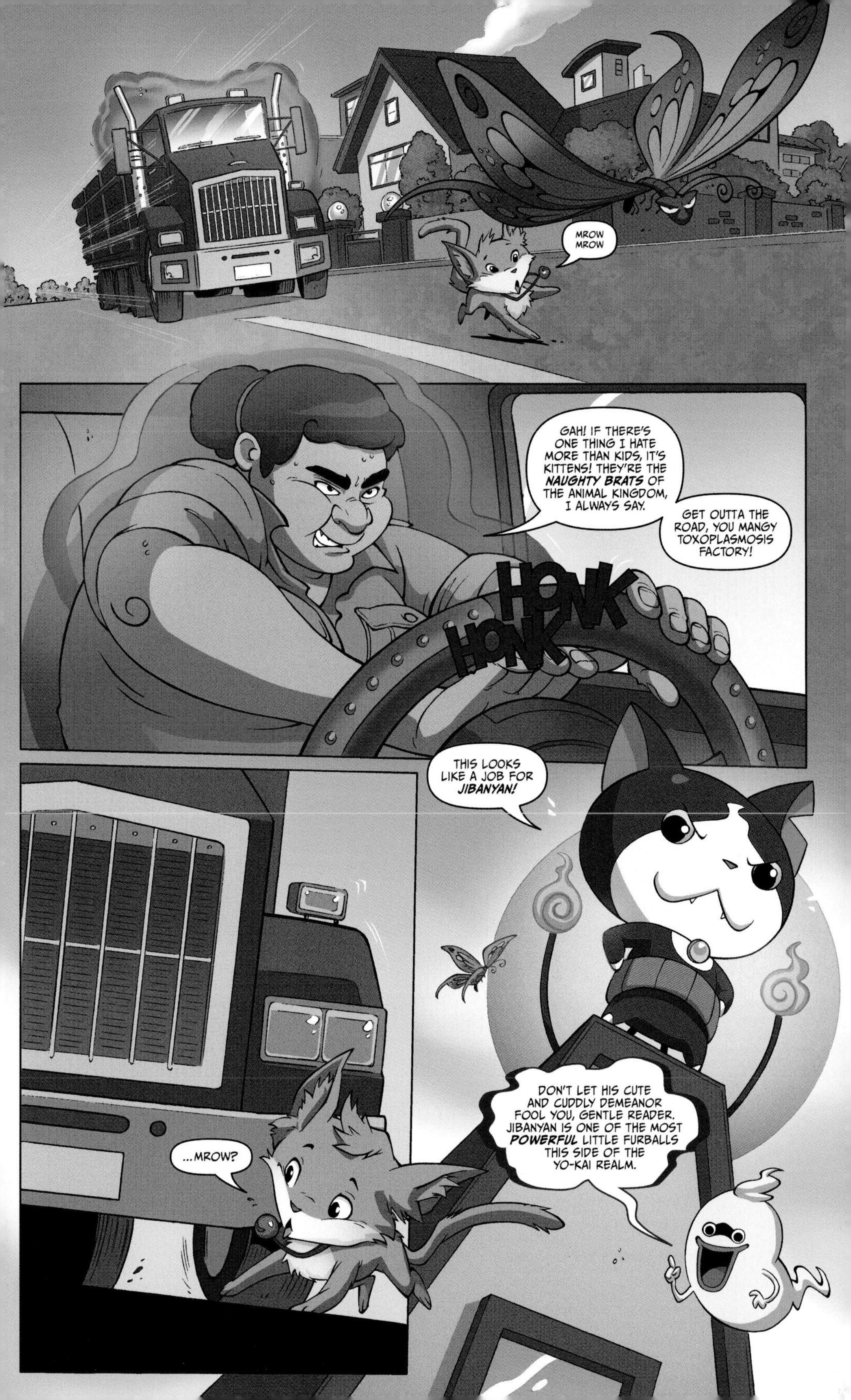
MROW MROW
GAH! IF THERE'S ONE THING I HATE MORE THAN KIDS, IT'S KITTENS! THEY'RE THE NAUGHTY BRATS OF THE ANIMAL KINGDOM, I ALWAYS SAY.
GET OUTTA THE ROAD, YOU MANGY TOXOPLASMOSIS FACTORY!
HONK HONK
THIS LOOKS LIKE A JOB FOR JIBANYAN!
...MROW?
DON'T LET HIS CUTE AND CUDDLY DEMEANOR FOOL YOU, GENTLE READER. JIBANYAN IS ONE OF THE MOST POWERFUL LITTLE FURBALLS THIS SIDE OF THE YO-KAI REALM.

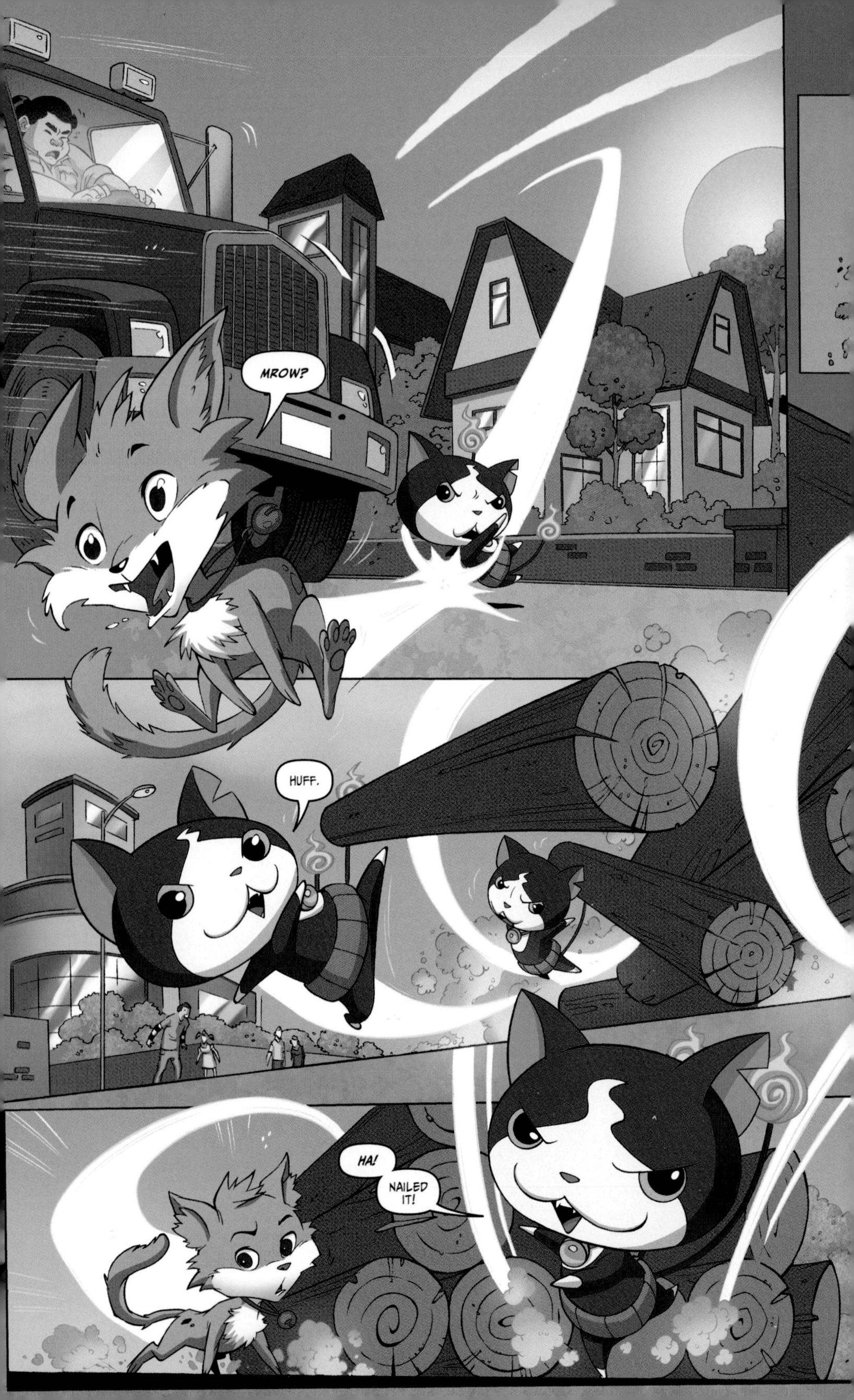
MROW?
HUFF.
HA!
NAILED IT!

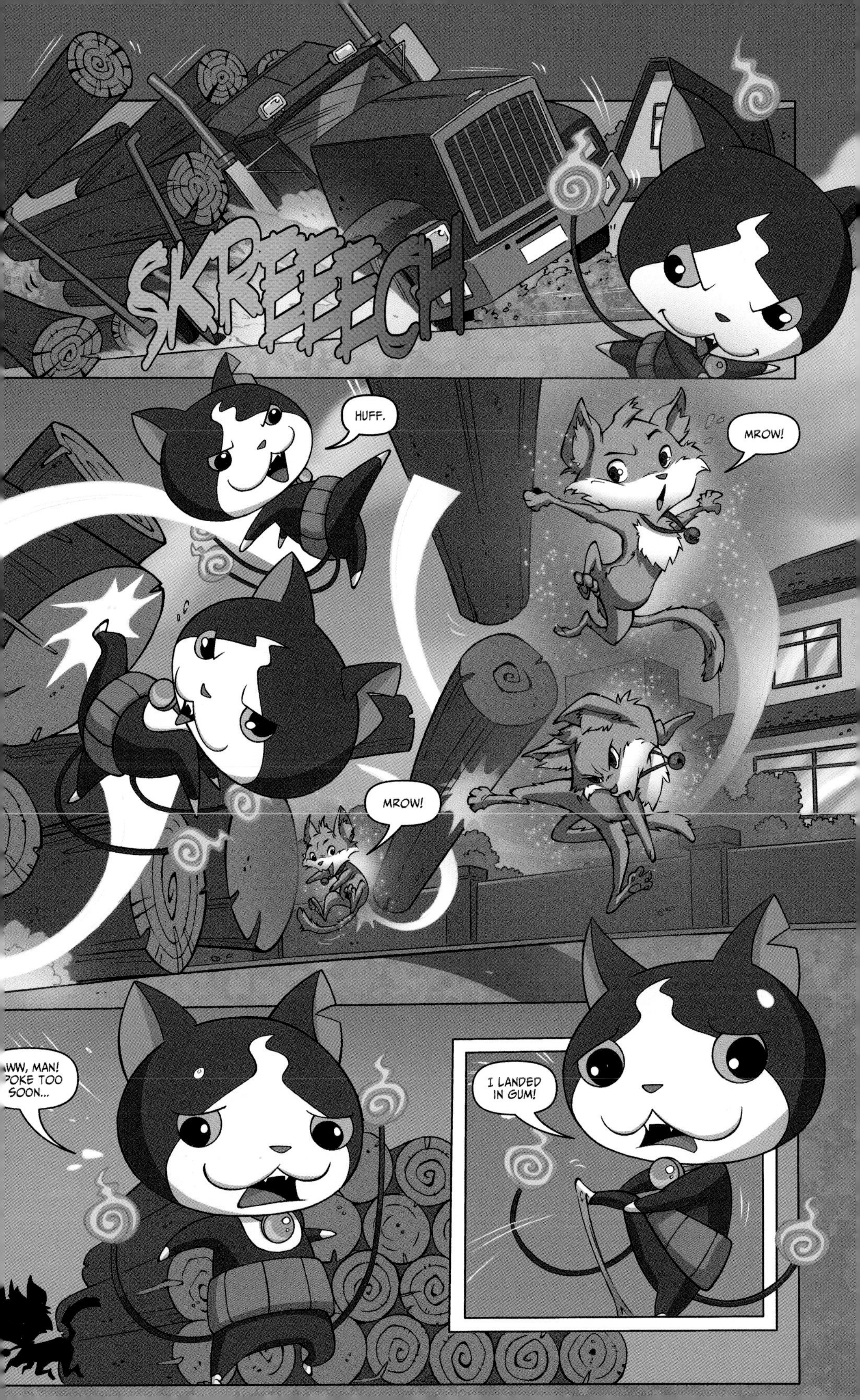
SKREEECH
HUFF.
MROW!
MROW!
AWW, MAN! SPOKE TOO SOON...
I LANDED IN GUM!

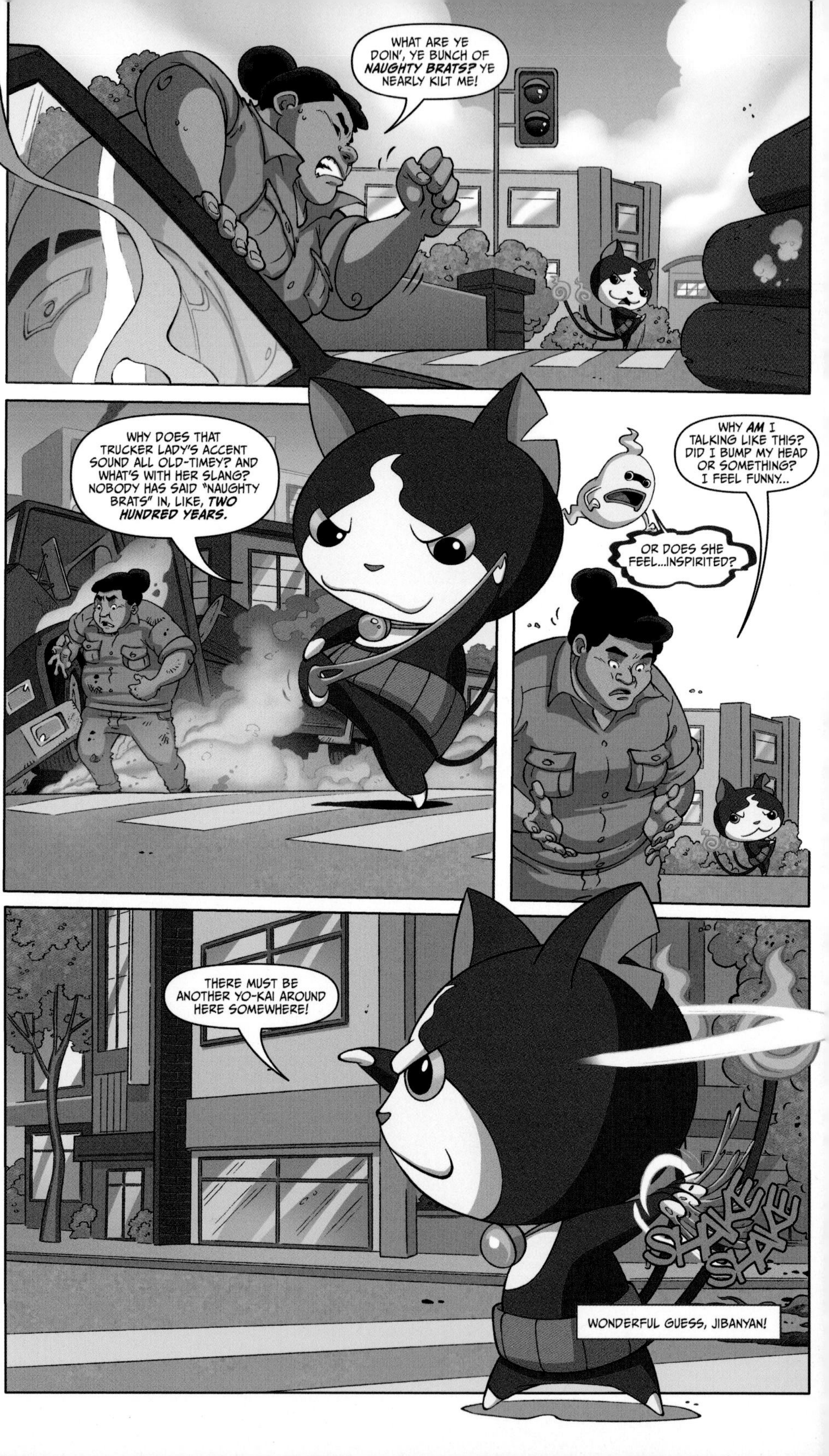
WHAT ARE YE DOIN', YE BUNCH OF NAUGHTY BRATS? YE NEARLY KILT ME!
WHY DOES THAT TRUCKER LADY'S ACCENT SOUND ALL OLD-TIMEY? AND WHAT'S WITH HER SLANG? NOBODY HAS SAID "NAUGHTY BRATS" IN, LIKE, TWO HUNDRED YEARS.
WHY AM I TALKING LIKE THIS? DID I BUMP MY HEAD OR SOMETHING? I FEEL FUNNY...
OR DOES SHE FEEL...INSPIRITED?
THERE MUST BE ANOTHER YO-KAI AROUND HERE SOMEWHERE!
SHAKE SHAKE
WONDERFUL GUESS, JIBANYAN!

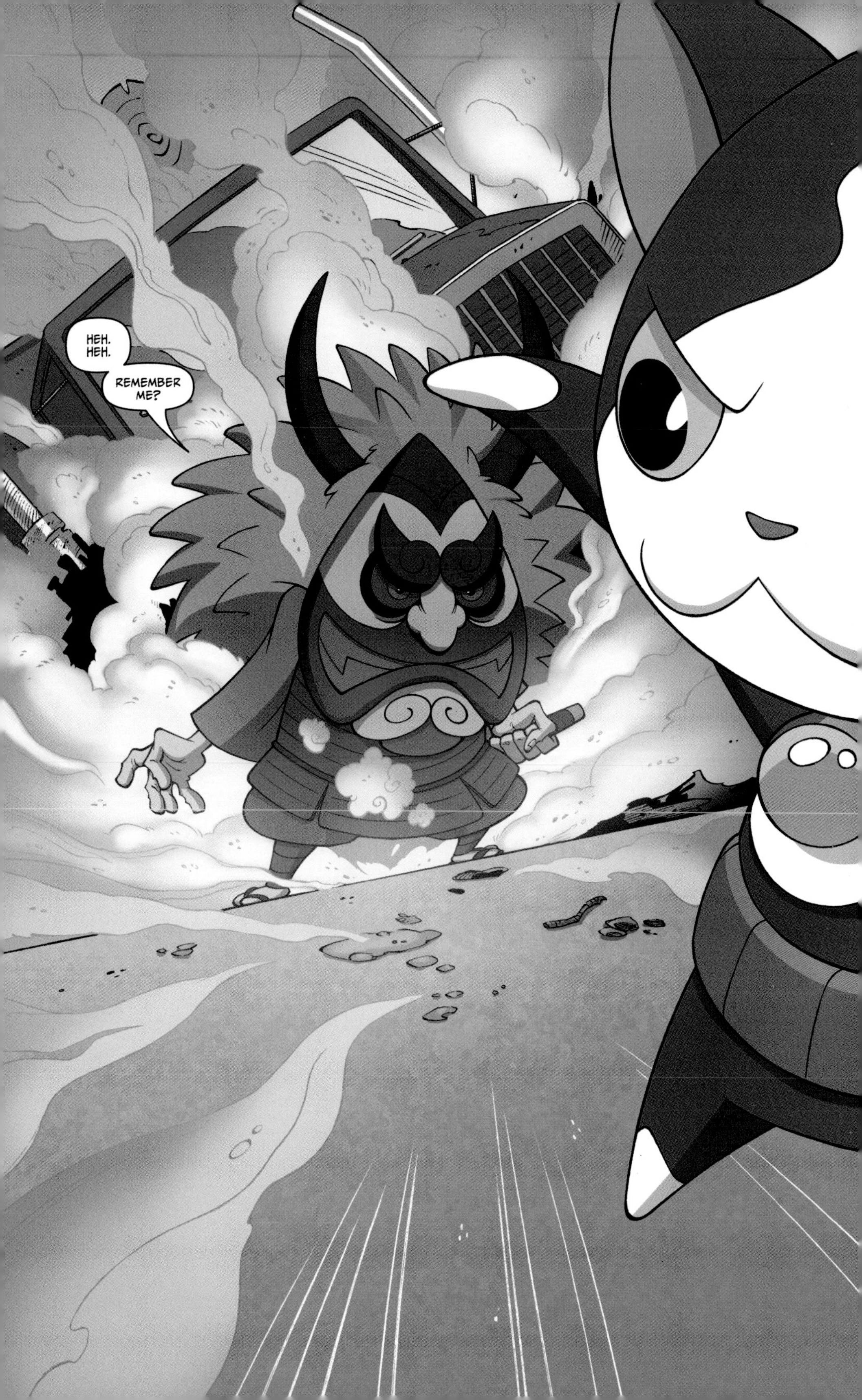
HEH.
HEH.
REMEMBER ME?

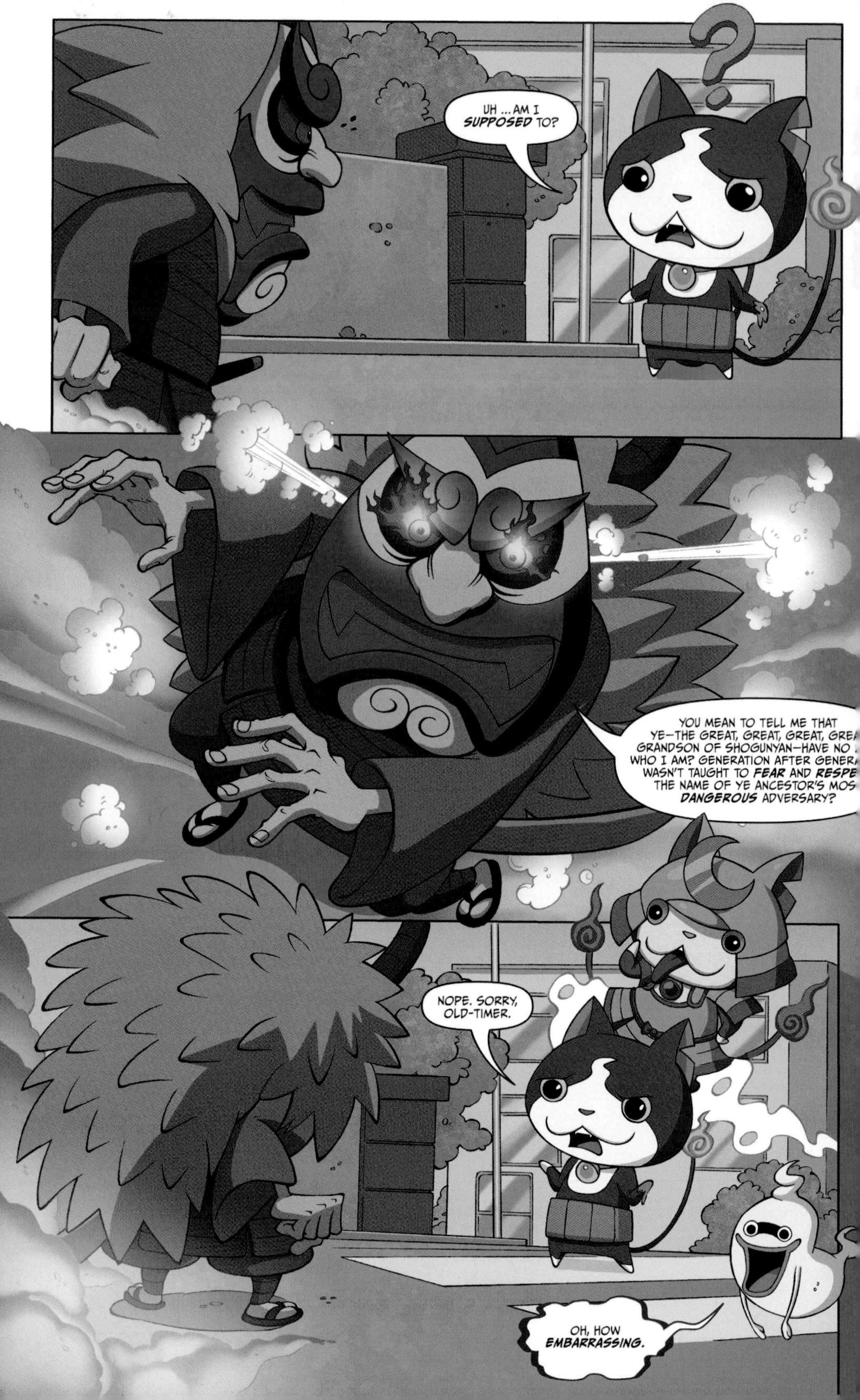
UH ... AM I SUPPOSED TO?
YOU MEAN TO TELL ME THAT YE—THE GREAT, GREAT, GREAT, GREA GRANDSON OF SHOGUNYAN—HAVE NO WHO I AM? GENERATION AFTER GENER WASN'T TAUGHT TO FEAR AND RESPE THE NAME OF YE ANCESTOR'S MOS DANGEROUS ADVERSARY?
NOPE. SORRY, OLD-TIMER.
OH, HOW EMBARRASSING.

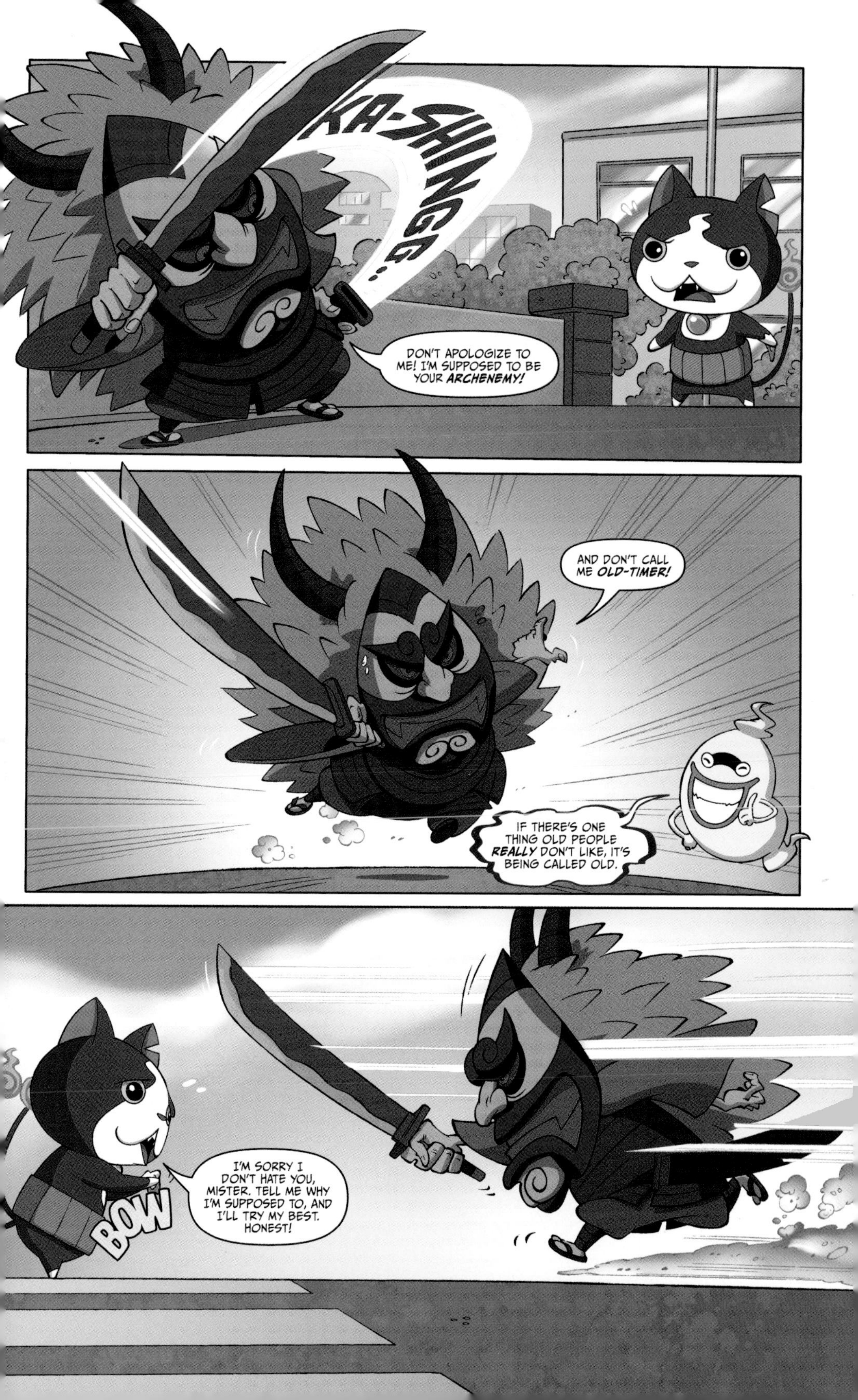
KA-SHINGG..
DON'T APOLOGIZE TO ME! I'M SUPPOSED TO BE YOUR ARCHENEMY!
AND DON'T CALL ME OLD-TIMER!
IF THERE'S ONE THING OLD PEOPLE REALLY DON'T LIKE, IT'S BEING CALLED OLD.
I'M SORRY I DON'T HATE YOU, MISTER. TELL ME WHY I'M SUPPOSED TO, AND I'LL TRY MY BEST. HONEST!
BOW

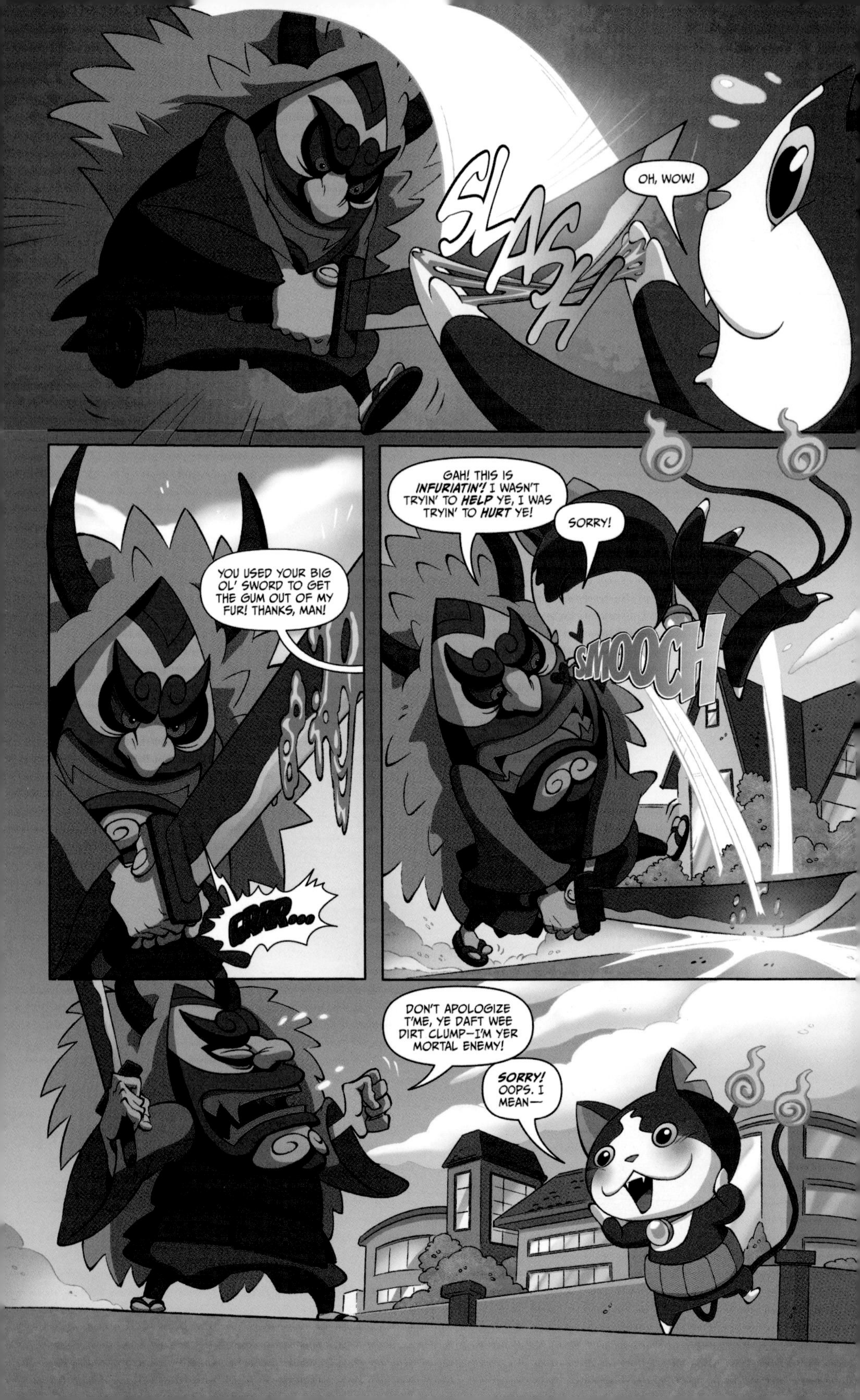
SLASH
OH, WOW!
YOU USED YOUR BIG OL' SWORD TO GET THE GUM OUT OF MY FUR! THANKS, MAN!
GRRR...
GAH! THIS IS INFURIATIN'! I WASN'T TRYIN' TO HELP YE, I WAS TRYIN' TO HURT YE!
SORRY!
SMOOCH
DON'T APOLOGIZE T'ME, YE DAFT WEE DIRT CLUMP—I'M YER MORTAL ENEMY!
SORRY! OOPS. I MEAN—

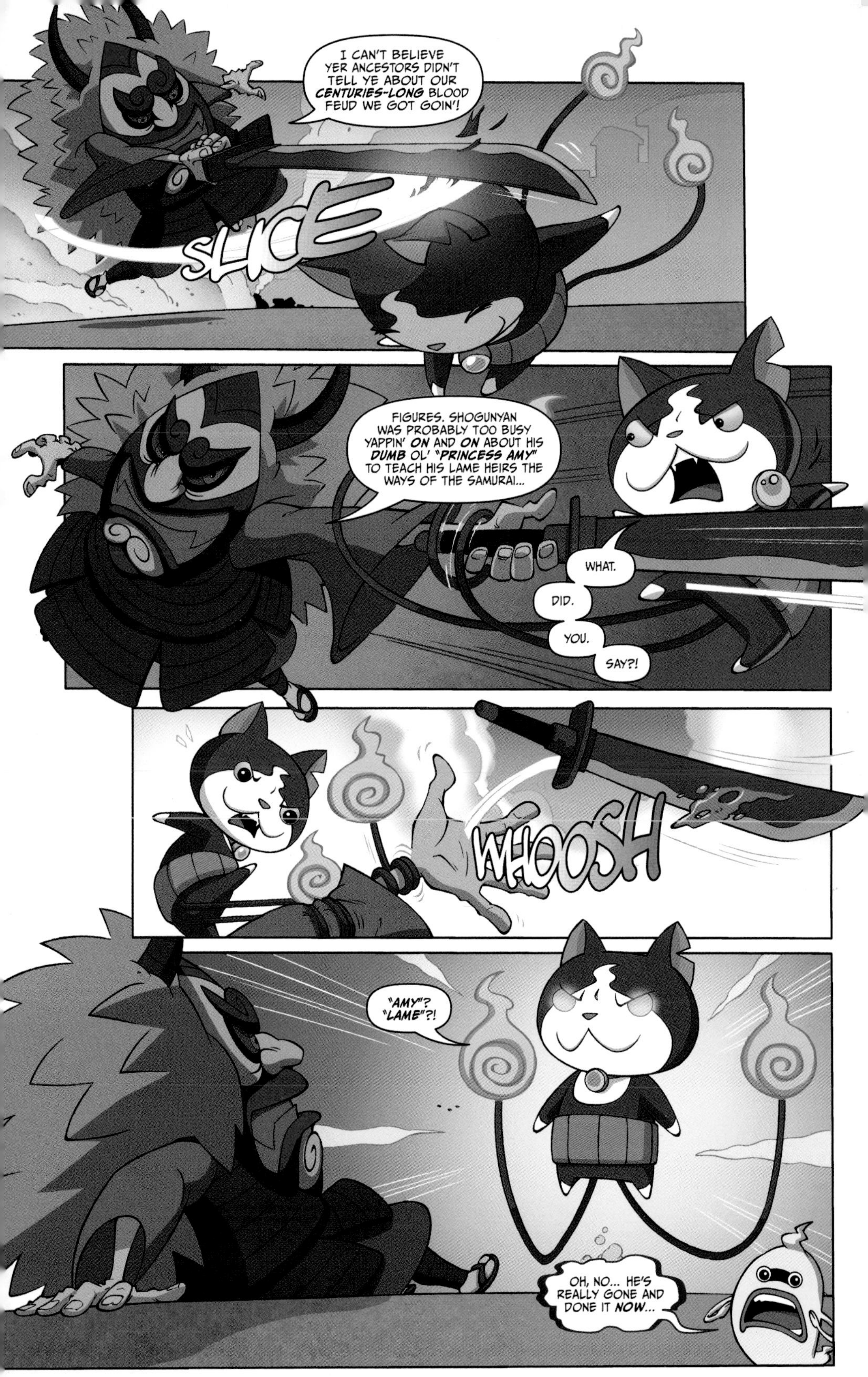
I CAN'T BELIEVE YER ANCESTORS DIDN'T TELL YE ABOUT OUR CENTURIES-LONG BLOOD FEUD WE GOT GOIN'!
SLICE
FIGURES. SHOGUNYAN WAS PROBABLY TOO BUSY YAPPIN' ON AND ON ABOUT HIS DUMB OL' "PRINCESS AMY" TO TEACH HIS LAME HEIRS THE WAYS OF THE SAMURAI...
WHAT.
DID.
YOU.
SAY?!
WHOOSH
"AMY"? "LAME"?!
...
OH, NO... HE'S REALLY GONE AND DONE IT NOW...

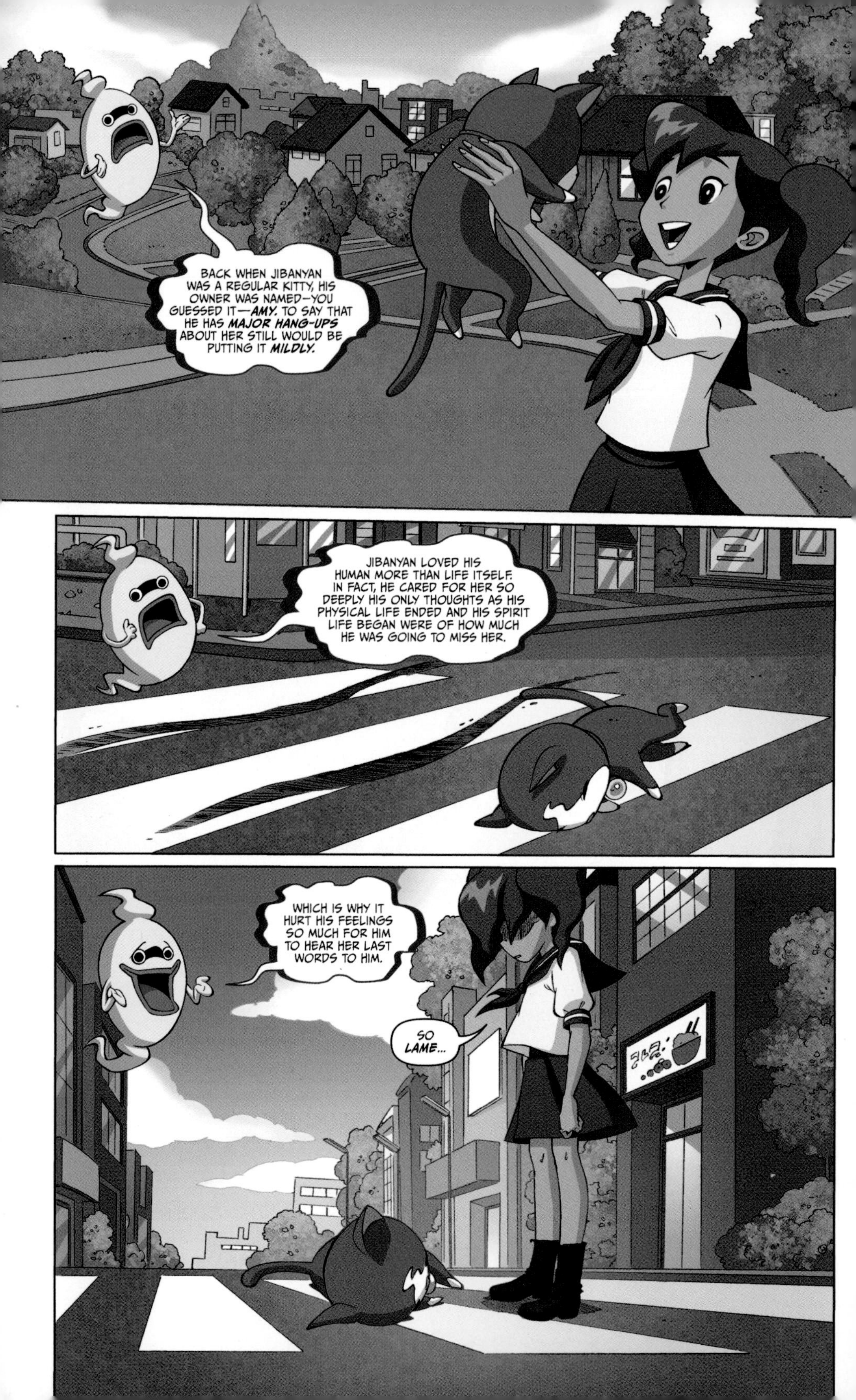
BACK WHEN JIBANYAN WAS A REGULAR KITTY, HIS OWNER WAS NAMED—YOU GUESSED IT—AMY. TO SAY THAT HE HAS MAJOR HANG-UPS ABOUT HER STILL WOULD BE PUTTING IT MILDLY.
JIBANYAN LOVED HIS HUMAN MORE THAN LIFE ITSELF. IN FACT, HE CARED FOR HER SO DEEPLY HIS ONLY THOUGHTS AS HIS PHYSICAL LIFE ENDED AND HIS SPIRIT LIFE BEGAN WERE OF HOW MUCH HE WAS GOING TO MISS HER.
WHICH IS WHY IT HURT HIS FEELINGS SO MUCH FOR HIM TO HEAR HER LAST WORDS TO HIM.
SO LAME...

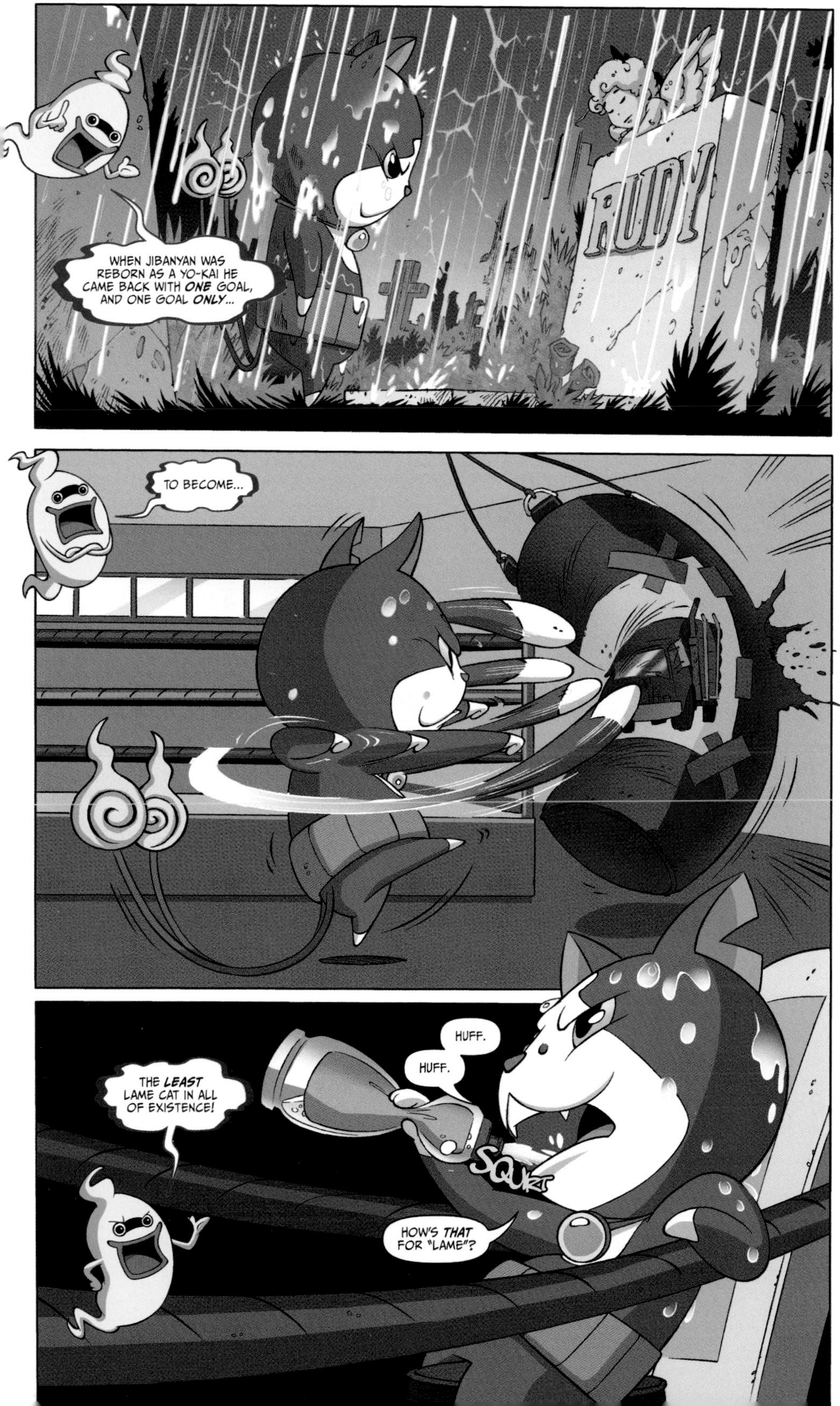
WHEN JIBANYAN WAS REBORN AS A YO-KAI HE CAME BACK WITH ONE GOAL, AND ONE GOAL ONLY...
RUDY
TO BECOME...
HUFF.
HUFF.
THE LEAST LAME CAT IN ALL OF EXISTENCE!
SQUIRT
HOW'S THAT FOR "LAME"?

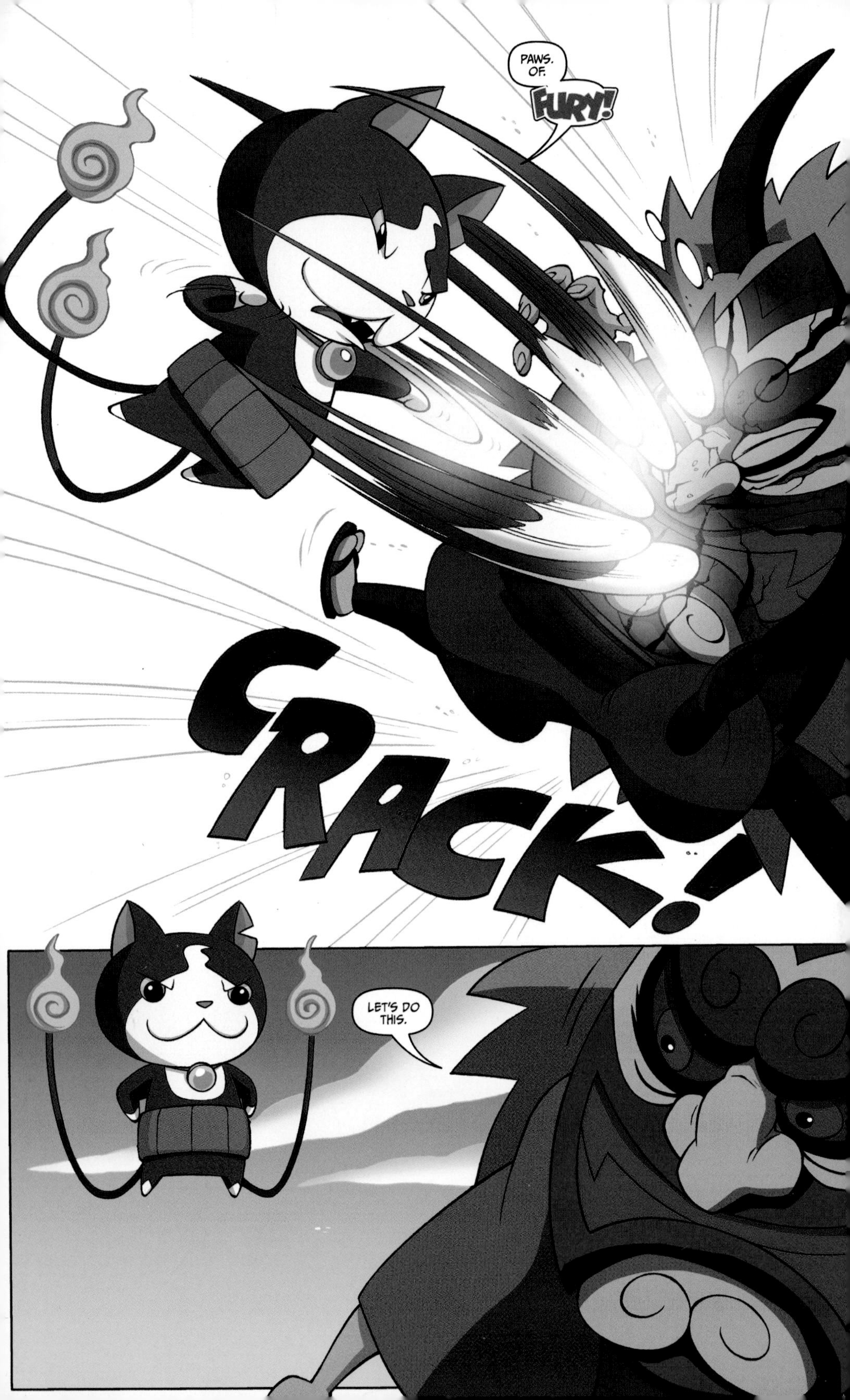
PAWS. OF. FURY!
CRACK!!
LET'S DO THIS.

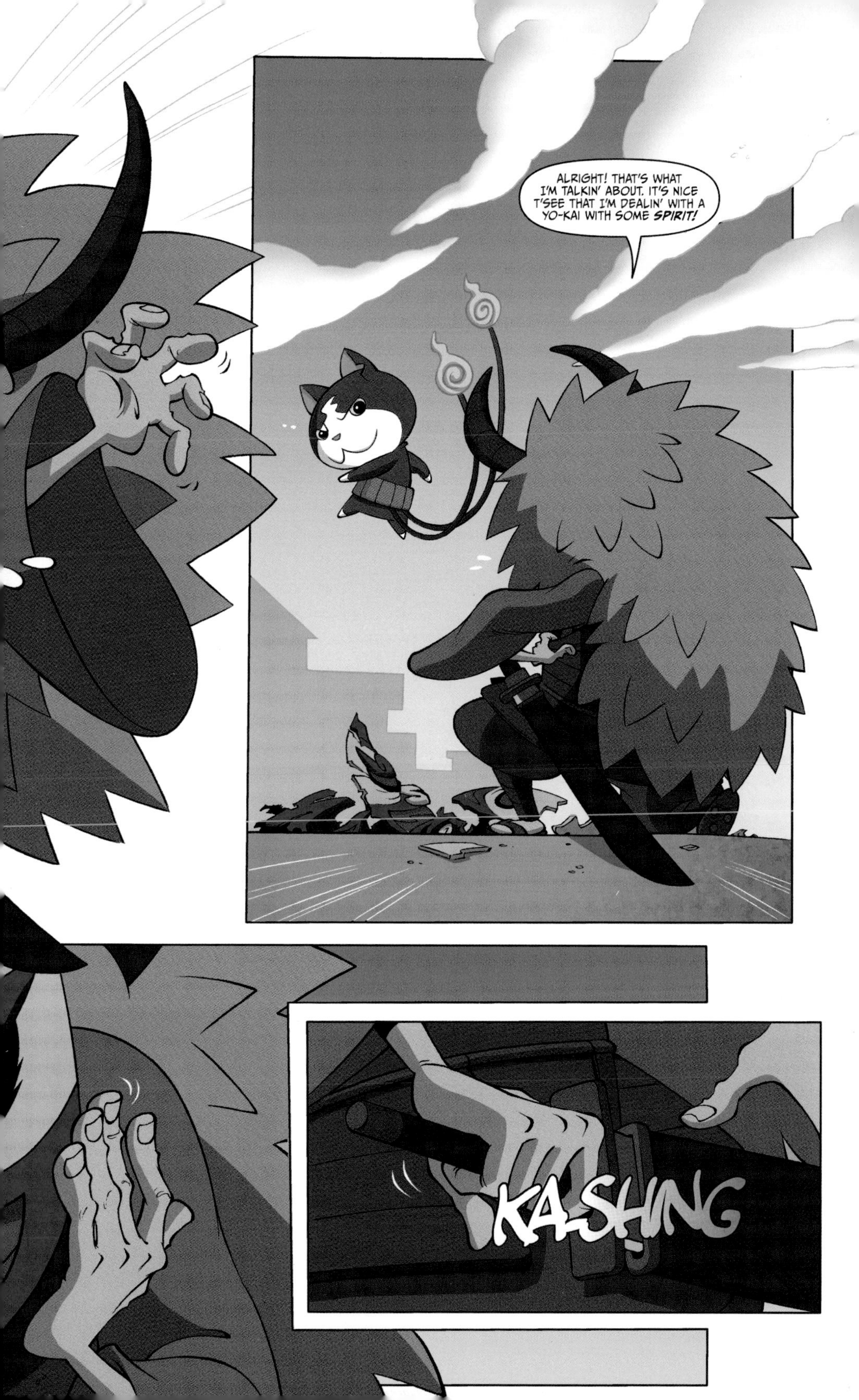
ALRIGHT! THAT'S WHAT I'M TALKIN' ABOUT. IT'S NICE T'SEE THAT I'M DEALIN' WITH A YO-KAI WITH SOME SPIRIT!
KA-SHING

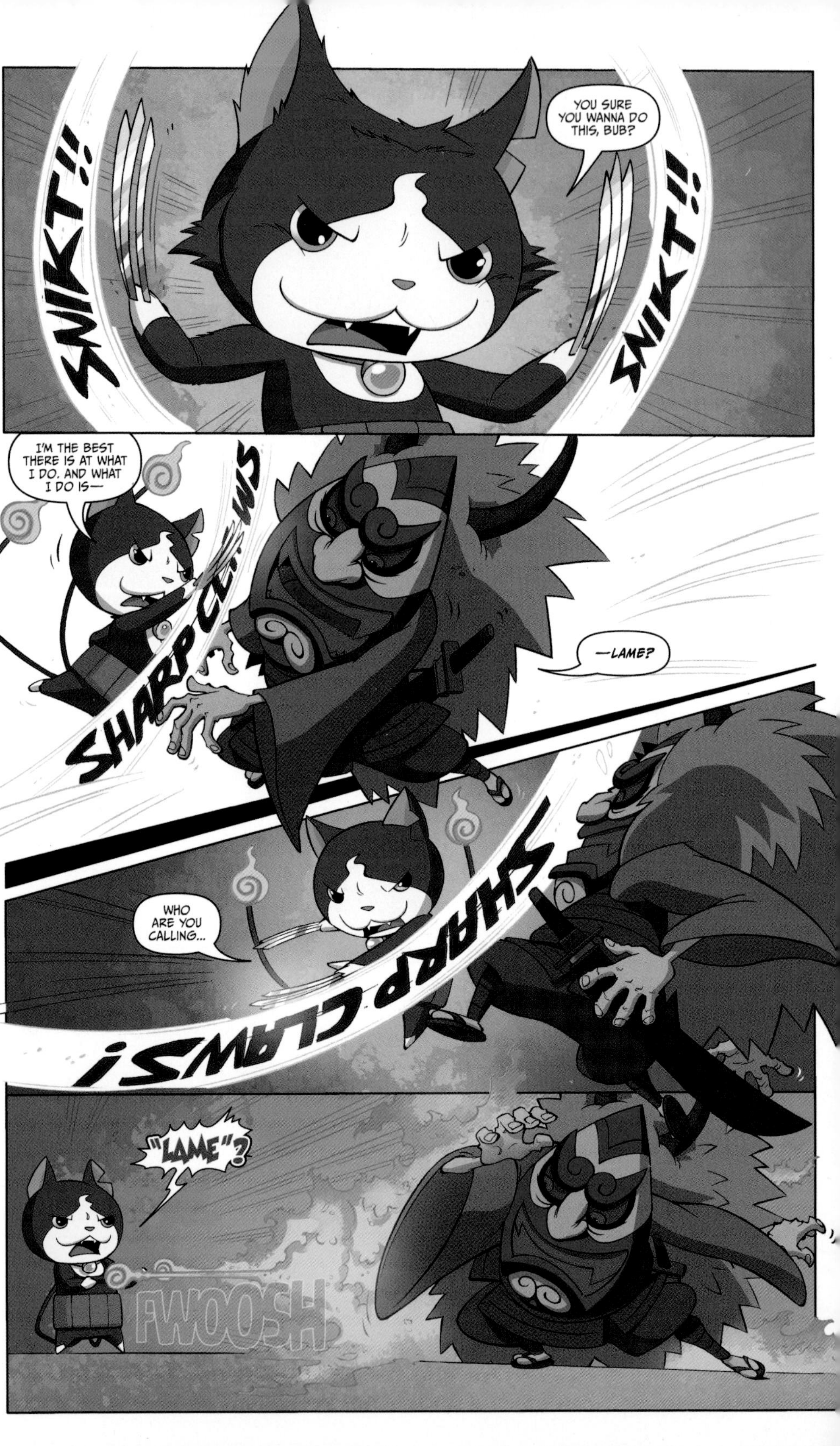
SNIKT!!
YOU SURE YOU WANNA DO THIS, BUB?
SNIKT!!
I'M THE BEST THERE IS AT WHAT I DO. AND WHAT I DO IS—
—LAME?
WHO ARE YOU CALLING...
SHARP CLAWS!
"LAME"?
FWOOSH

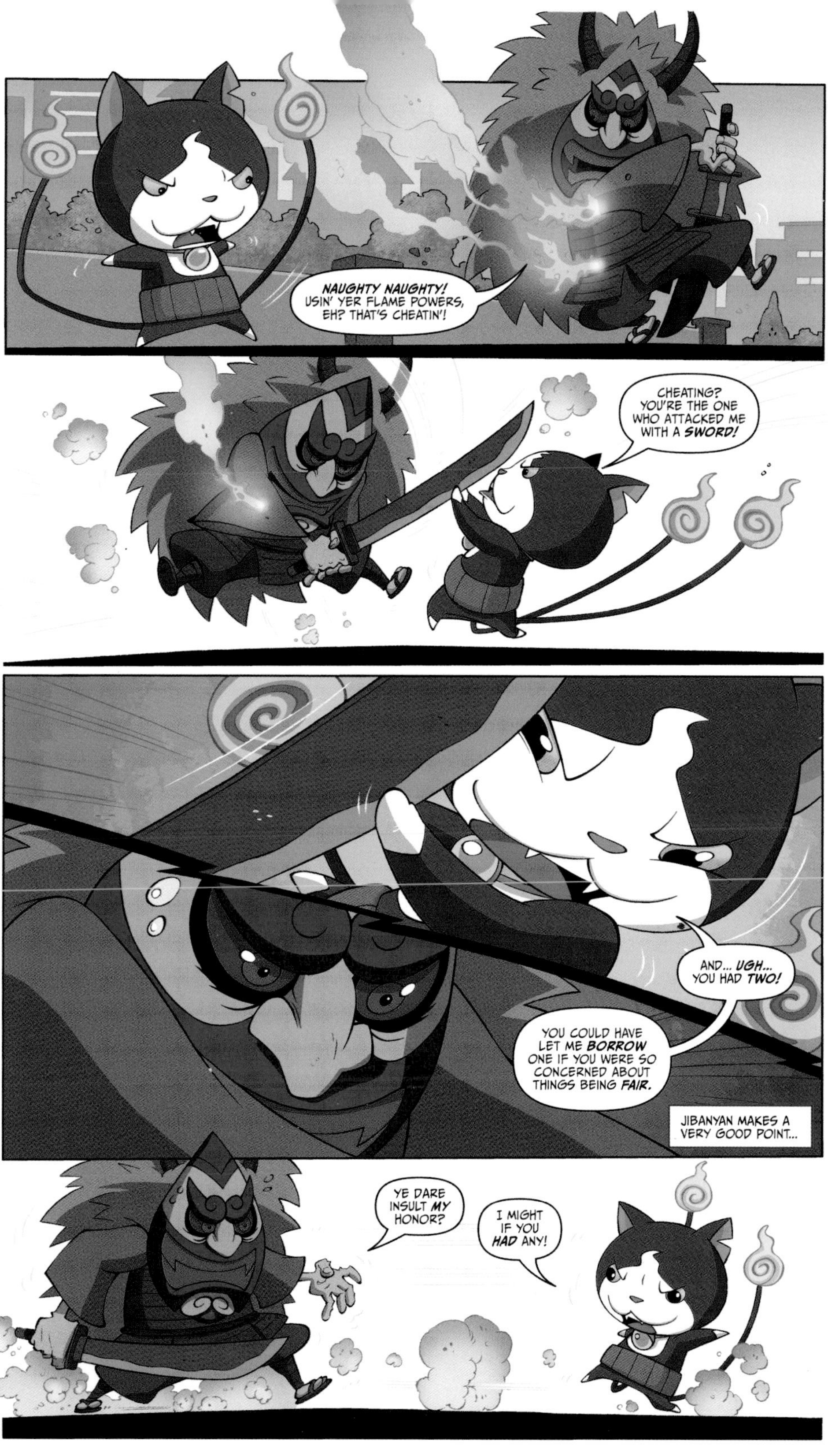
NAUGHTY NAUGHTY! USIN' YER FLAME POWERS, EH? THAT'S CHEATIN'!
CHEATING? YOU'RE THE ONE WHO ATTACKED ME WITH A SWORD!
AND... UGH... YOU HAD TWO!
YOU COULD HAVE LET ME BORROW ONE IF YOU WERE SO CONCERNED ABOUT THINGS BEING FAIR.
JIBANYAN MAKES A VERY GOOD POINT...
YE DARE INSULT MY HONOR?
I MIGHT IF YOU HAD ANY!

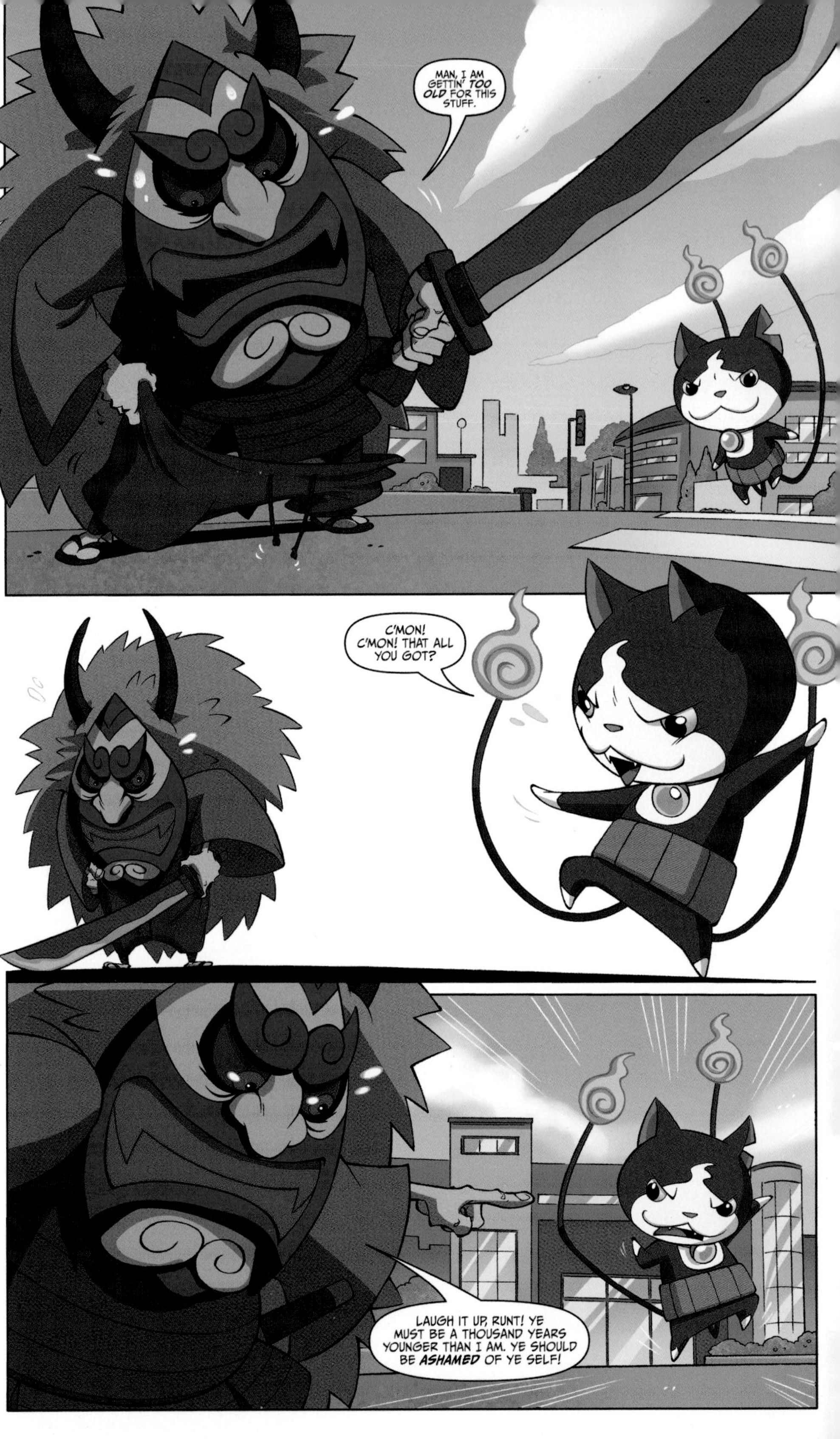
MAN, I AM GETTIN' TOO OLD FOR THIS STUFF.
C'MON! C'MON! THAT ALL YOU GOT?
LAUGH IT UP, RUNT! YE MUST BE A THOUSAND YEARS YOUNGER THAN I AM. YE SHOULD BE ASHAMED OF YE SELF!

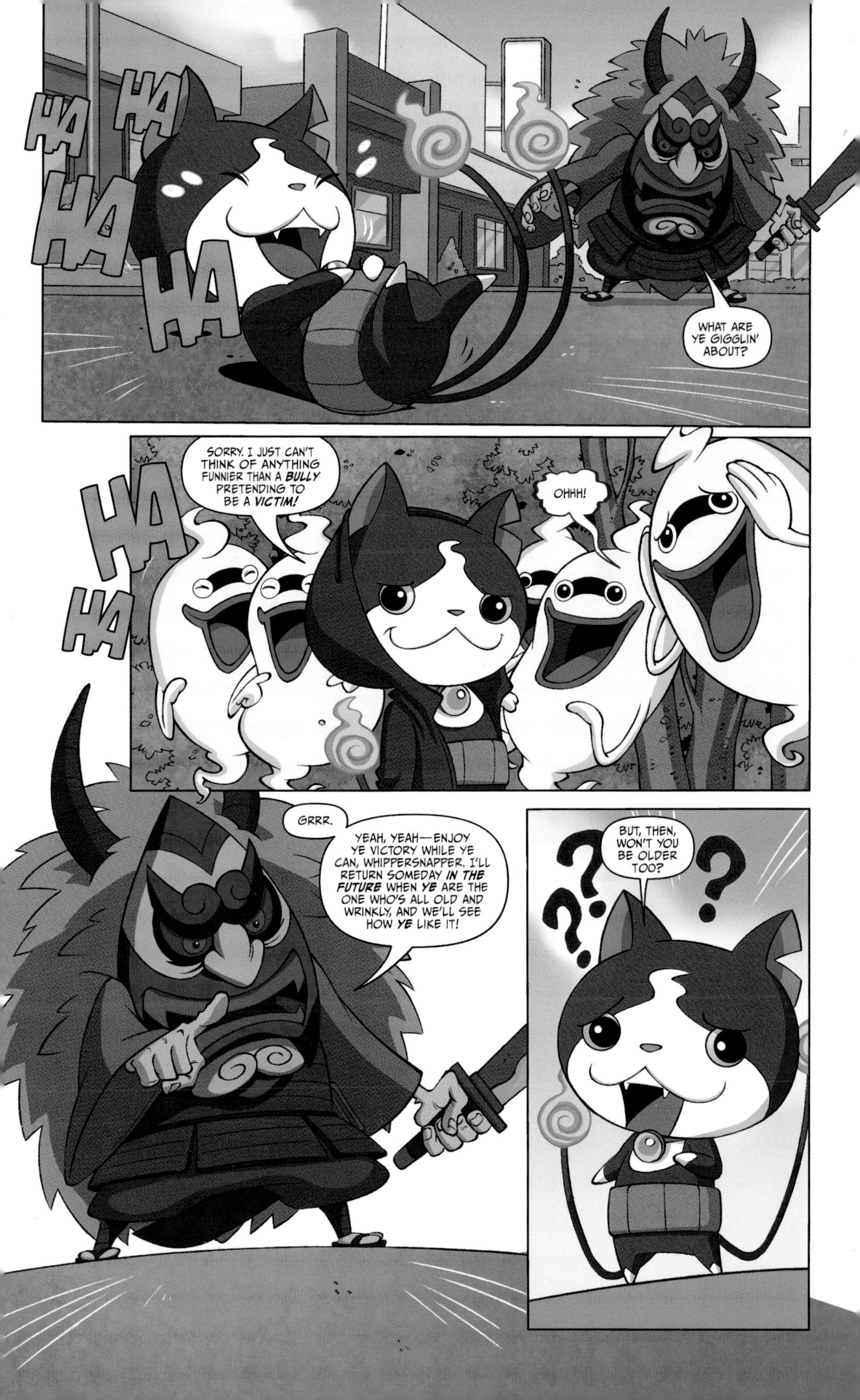
HA HA HA HA
WHAT ARE YE GIGGLIN' ABOUT?
HA HA
SORRY. I JUST CAN'T THINK OF ANYTHING FUNNIER THAN A BULLY PRETENDING TO BE A VICTIM!
OHHH!
GRRR.
YEAH, YEAH—ENJOY YE VICTORY WHILE YE CAN, WHIPPERSNAPPER. I'LL RETURN SOMEDAY IN THE FUTURE WHEN YE ARE THE ONE WHO'S ALL OLD AND WRINKLY, AND WE'LL SEE HOW YE LIKE IT!
BUT, THEN, WON'T YOU BE OLDER TOO?

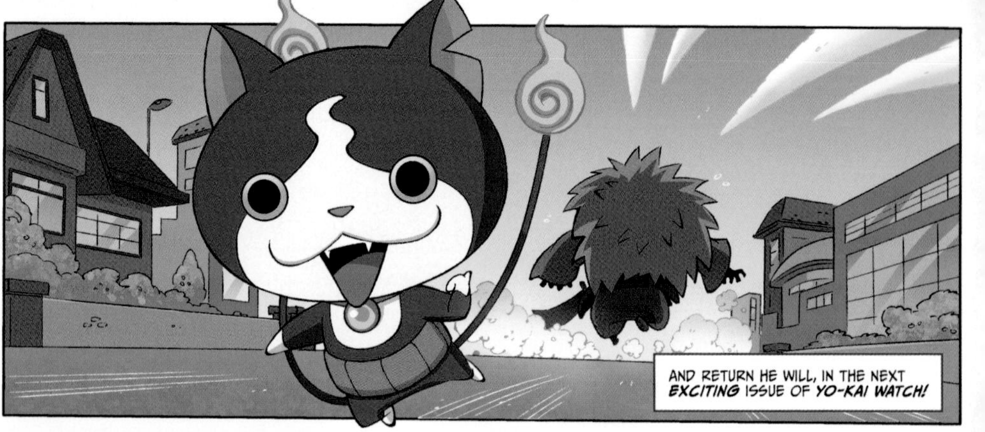
AND RETURN HE WILL, IN THE NEXT *EXCITING* ISSUE OF *YO-KAI WATCH!*

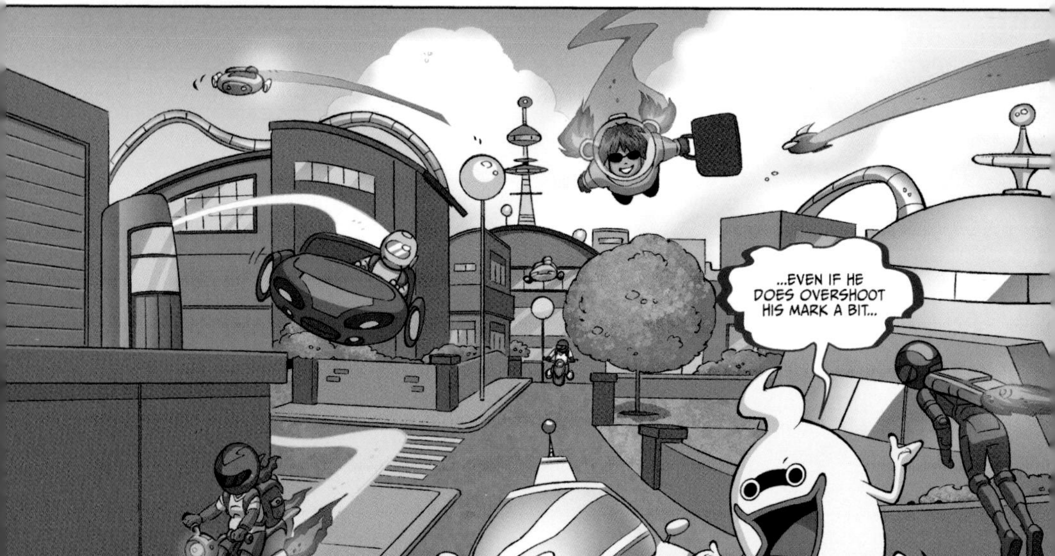
...EVEN IF HE DOES OVERSHOOT HIS MARK A BIT...

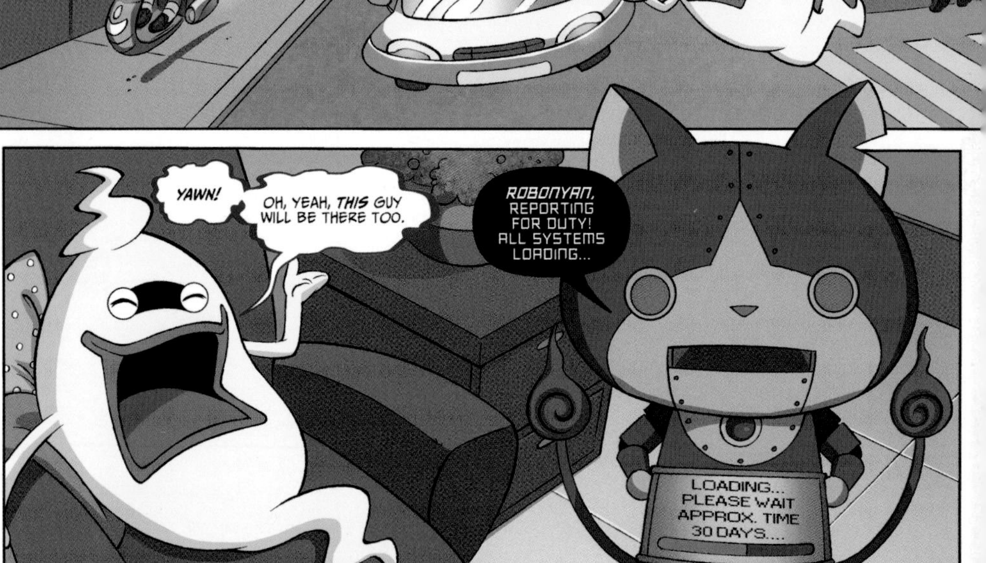
YAWN!
OH, YEAH, *THIS* GUY WILL BE THERE TOO.
ROBONYAN, REPORTING FOR DUTY! ALL SYSTEMS LOADING...
LOADING... PLEASE WAIT APPROX. TIME 30 DAYS....

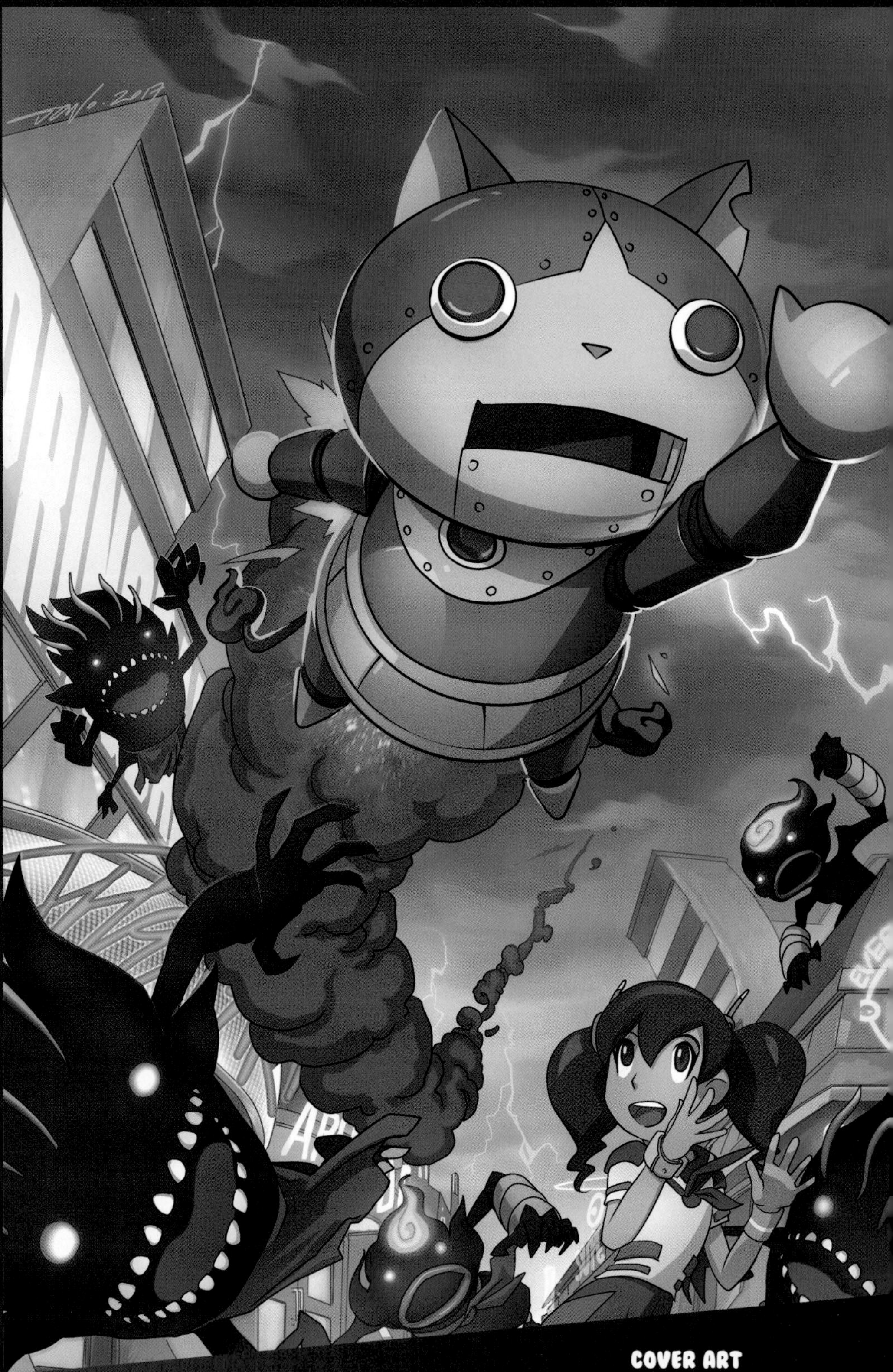

COVER ART
DONO SACHNEZ ALMARA

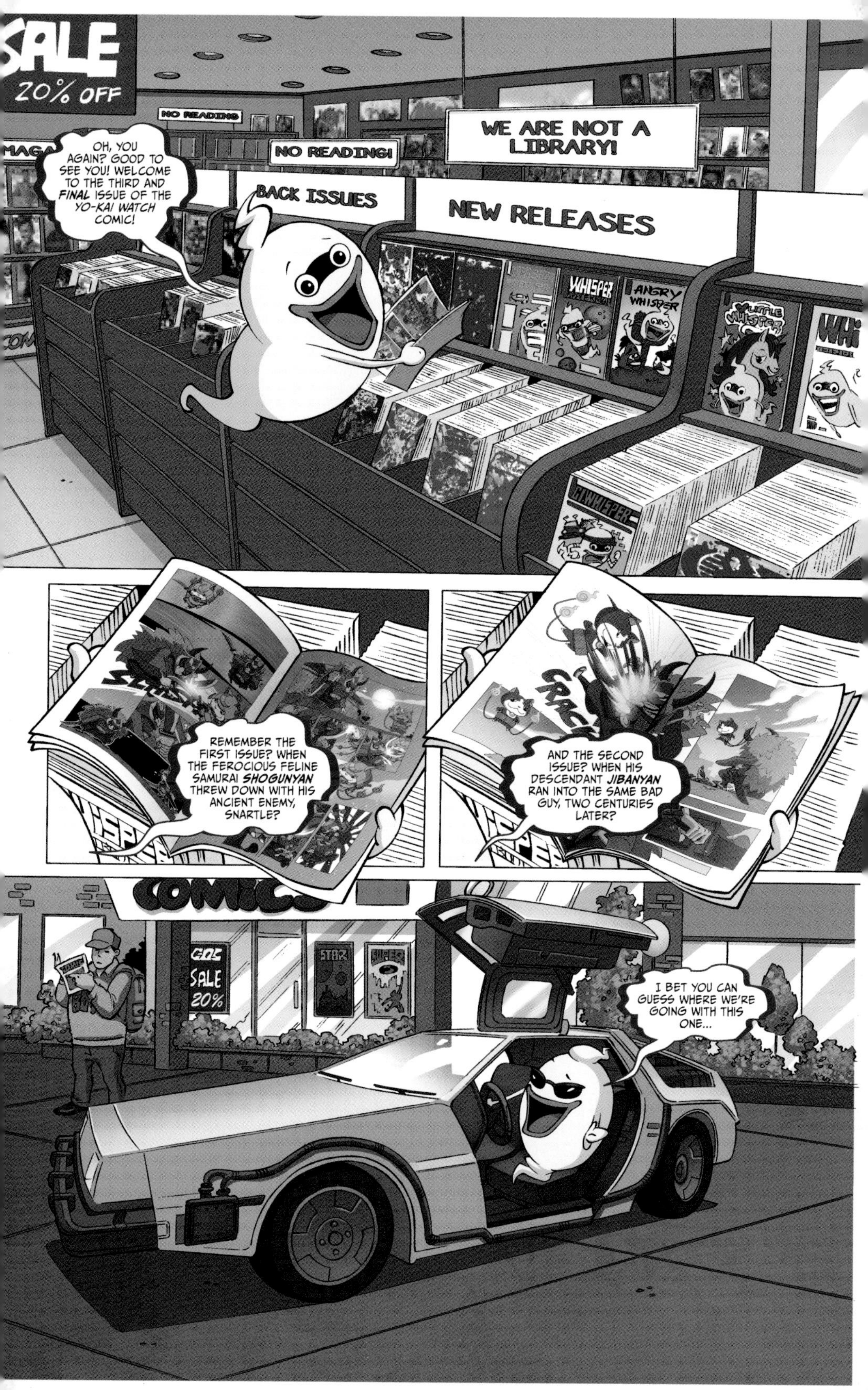
SALE
20% OFF
NO READING
NO READING!
WE ARE NOT A LIBRARY!
BACK ISSUES
NEW RELEASES
OH, YOU AGAIN? GOOD TO SEE YOU! WELCOME TO THE THIRD AND FINAL ISSUE OF THE YO-KAI WATCH COMIC!
WHISPER
ANGRY WHISPER
REMEMBER THE FIRST ISSUE? WHEN THE FEROCIOUS FELINE SAMURAI SHOGUNYAN THREW DOWN WITH HIS ANCIENT ENEMY, SNARTLE?
AND THE SECOND ISSUE? WHEN HIS DESCENDANT JIBANYAN RAN INTO THE SAME BAD GUY, TWO CENTURIES LATER?
COMICS
SALE
20%
STAR
SUPER
I BET YOU CAN GUESS WHERE WE'RE GOING WITH THIS ONE...

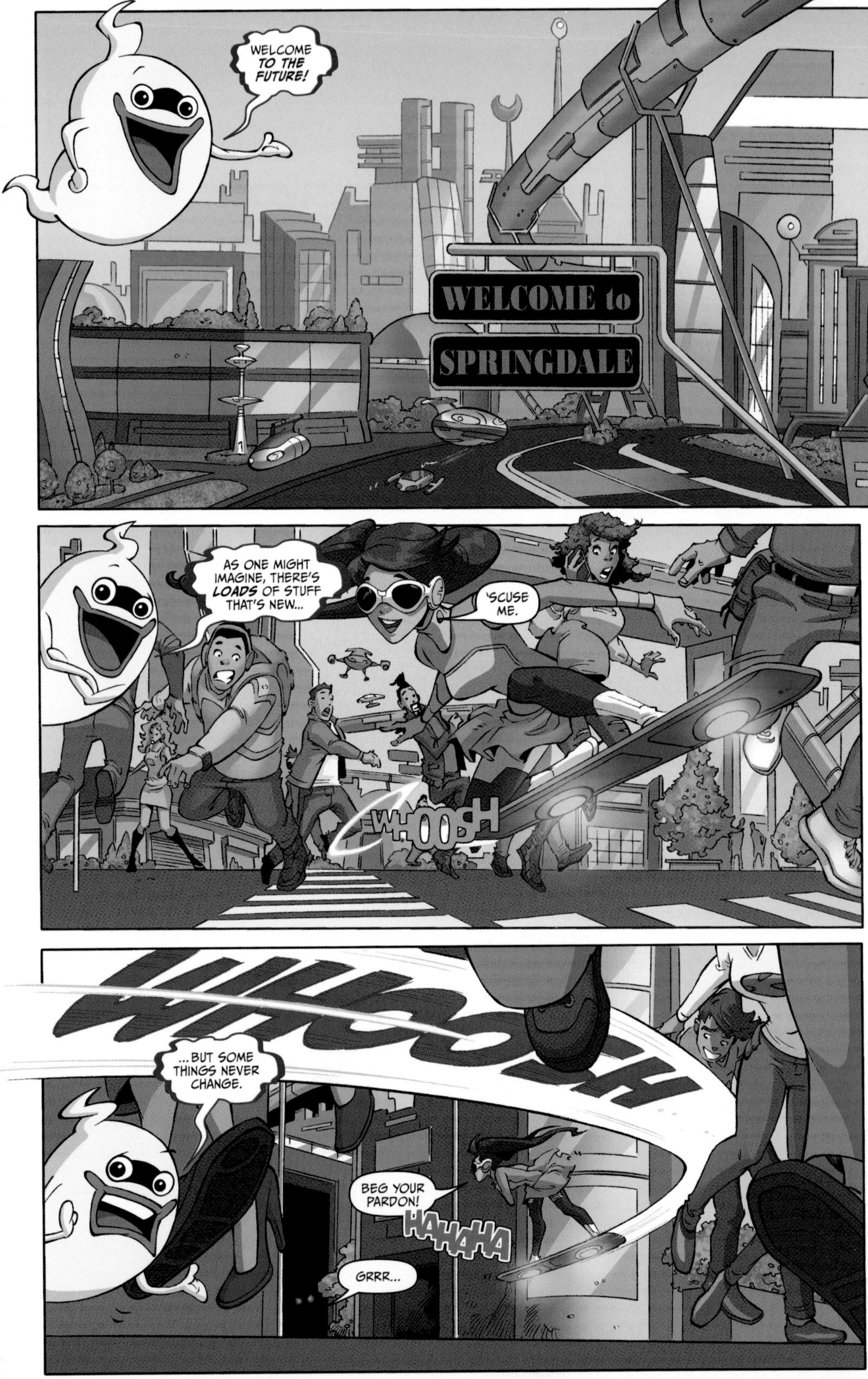
WELCOME TO THE FUTURE!
WELCOME to SPRINGDALE
AS ONE MIGHT IMAGINE, THERE'S LOADS OF STUFF THAT'S NEW...
'SCUSE ME.
WHOOSH
WHOOSH
...BUT SOME THINGS NEVER CHANGE.
BEG YOUR PARDON!
HAHAHA
GRRR...

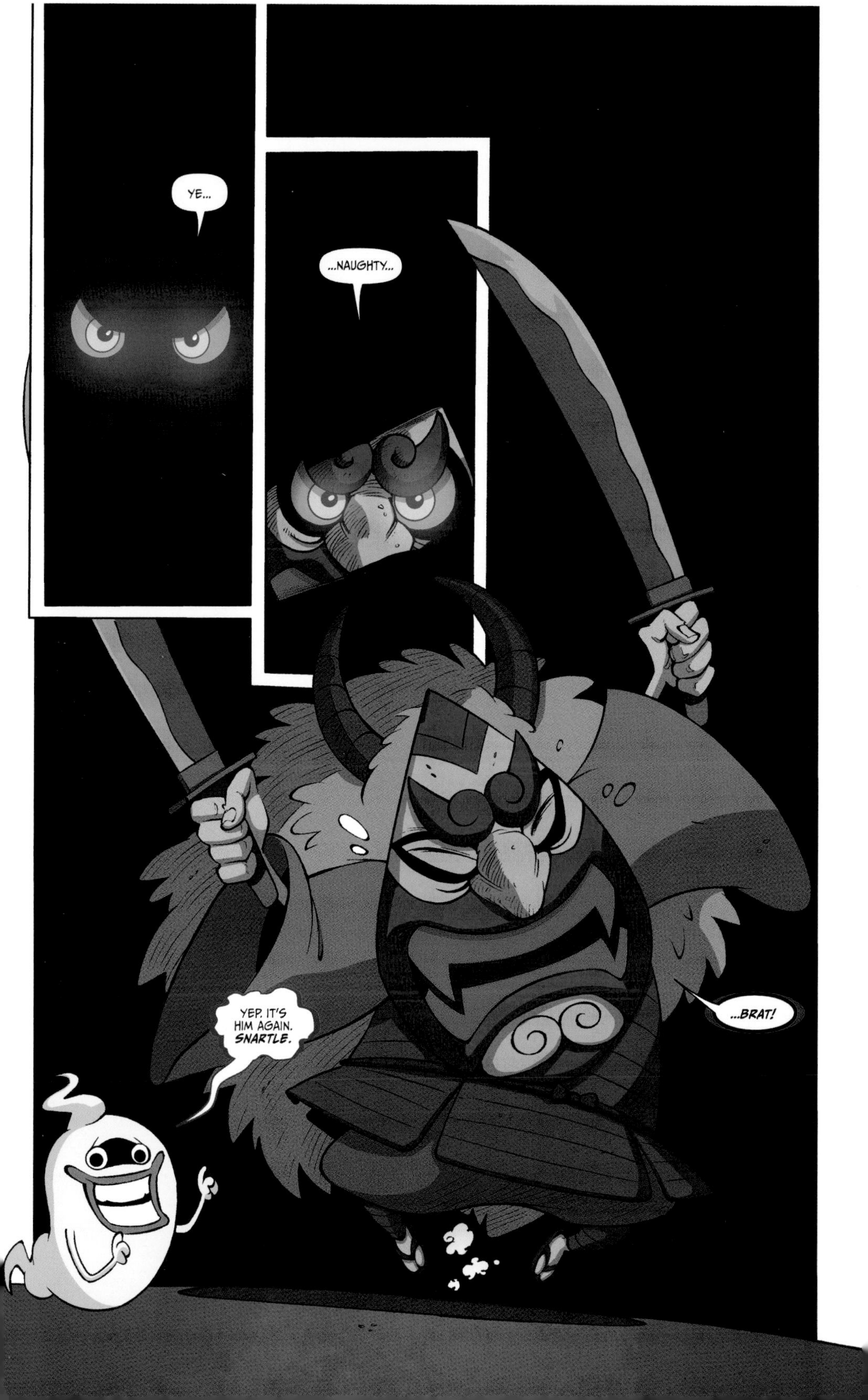
YE...
...NAUGHTY...
...BRAT!
YEP. IT'S HIM AGAIN. SNARTLE.

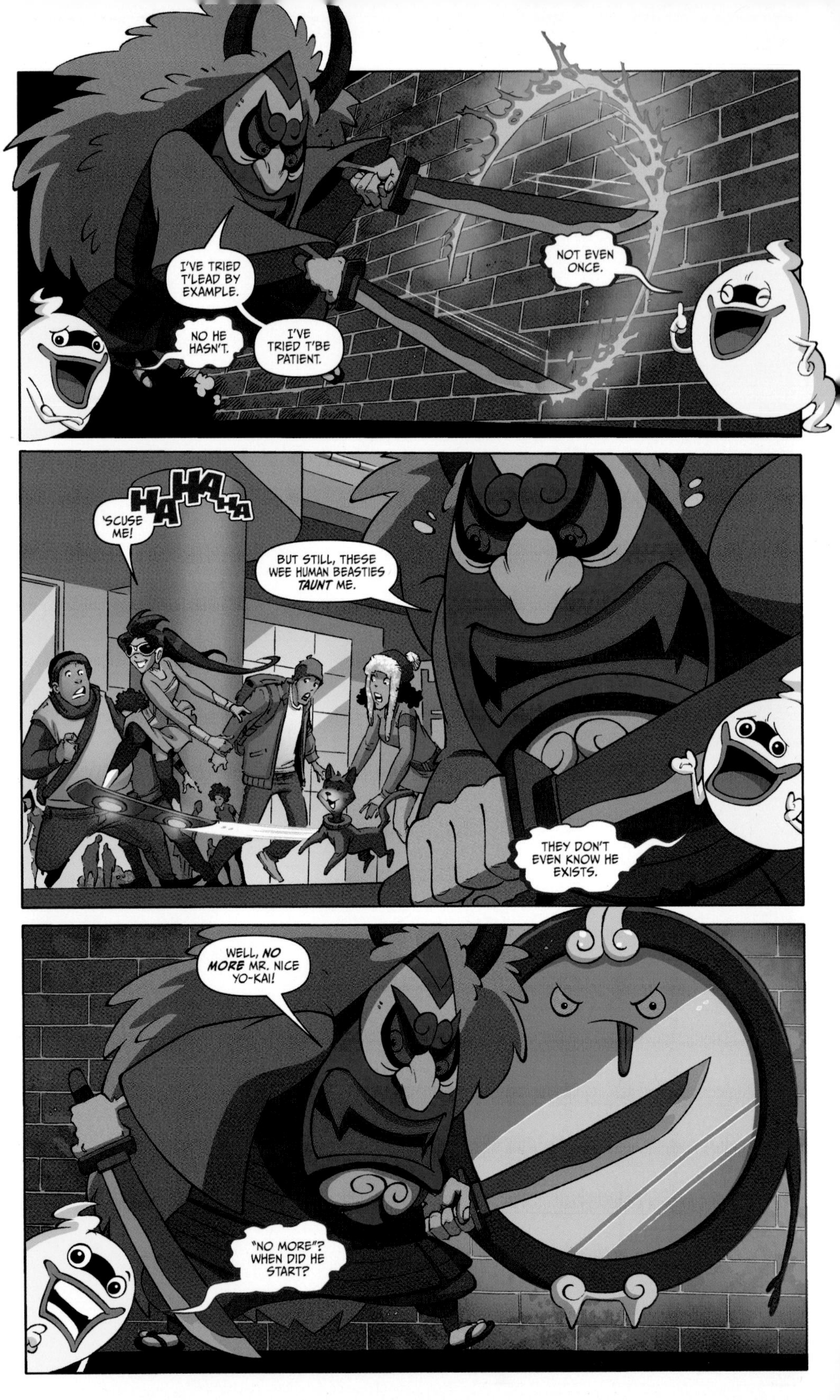
I'VE TRIED T'LEAD BY EXAMPLE.
NO HE HASN'T.
I'VE TRIED T'BE PATIENT.
NOT EVEN ONCE.
'SCUSE ME!
HA HA HA HA
BUT STILL, THESE WEE HUMAN BEASTIES TAUNT ME.
THEY DON'T EVEN KNOW HE EXISTS.
WELL, NO MORE MR. NICE YO-KAI!
"NO MORE"? WHEN DID HE START?

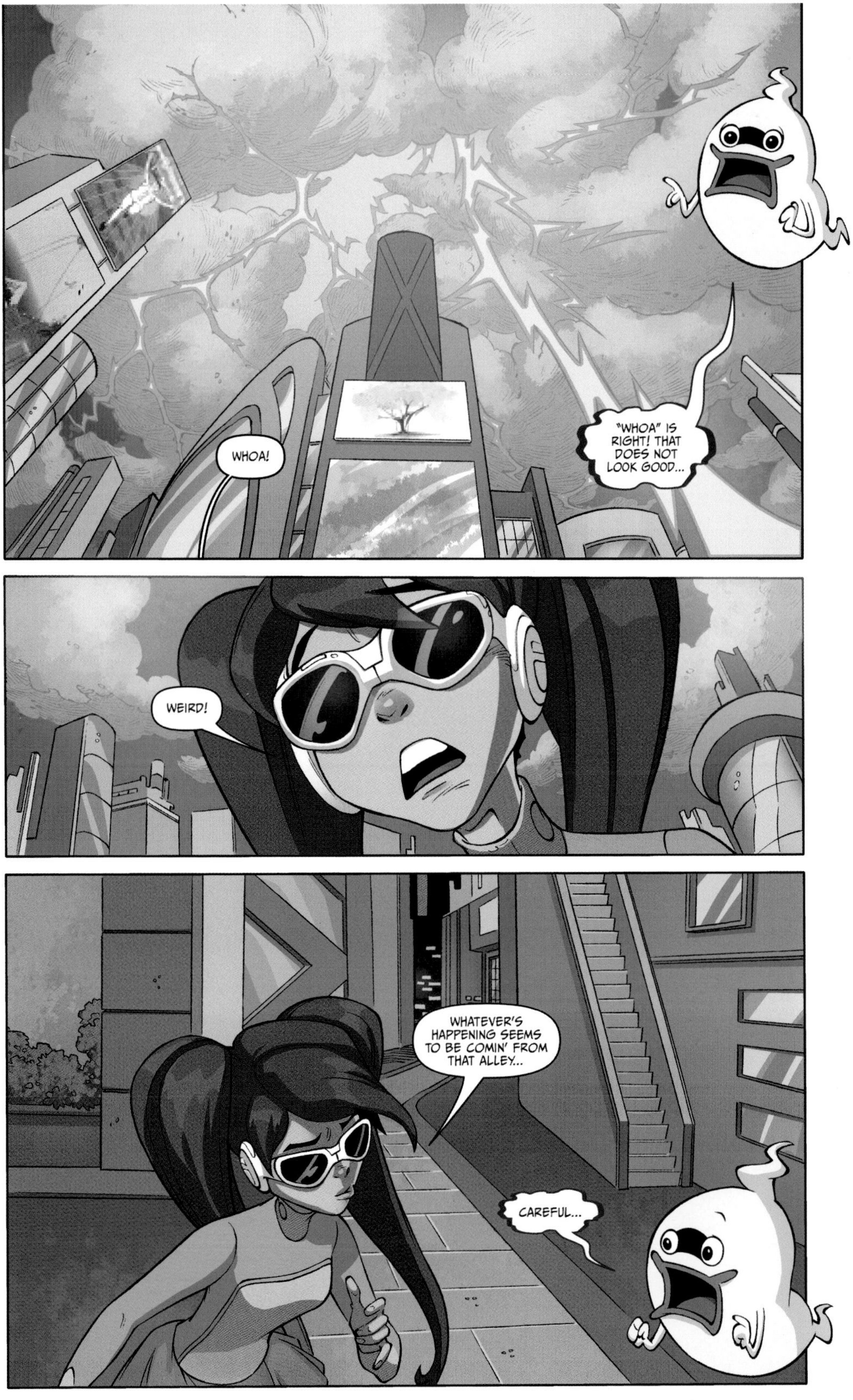
WHOA!
"WHOA" IS RIGHT! THAT DOES NOT LOOK GOOD...
WEIRD!
WHATEVER'S HAPPENING SEEMS TO BE COMIN' FROM THAT ALLEY...
CAREFUL...

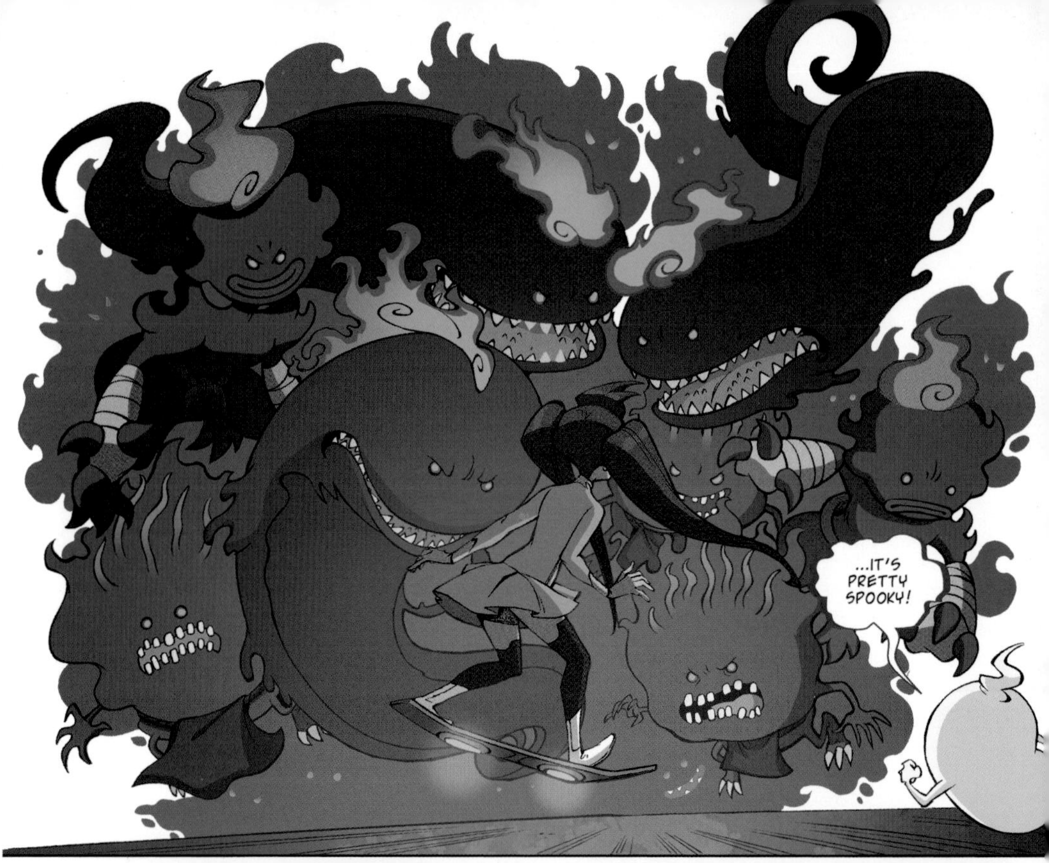
...IT'S PRETTY SPOOKY!

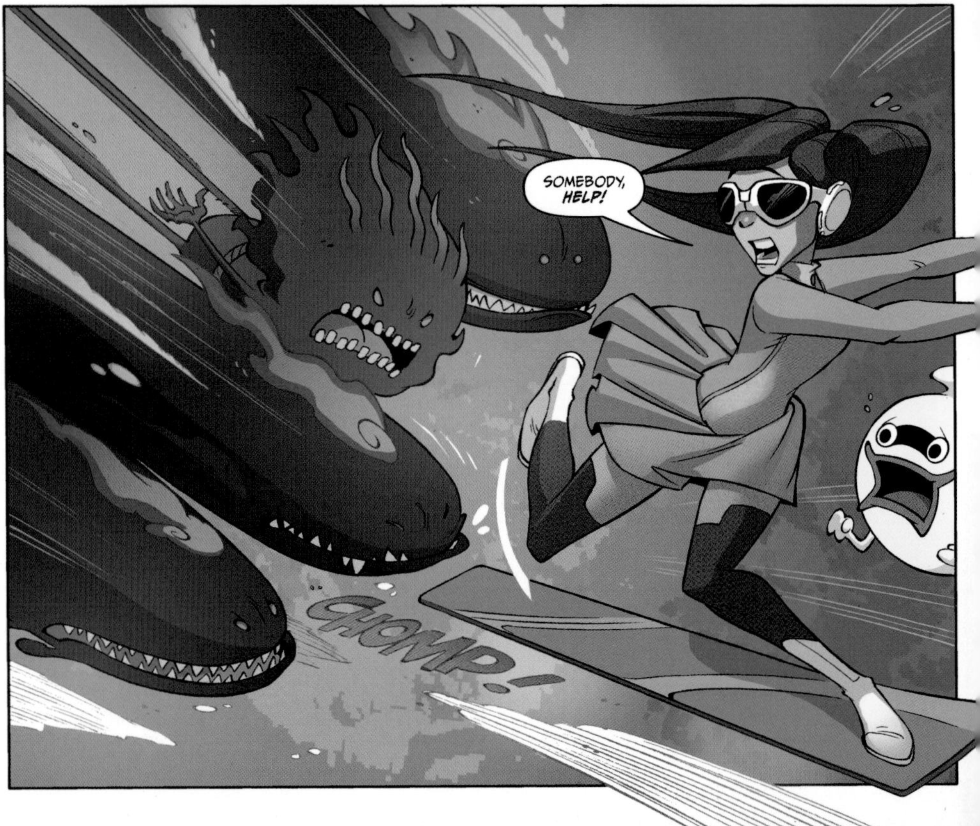
SOMEBODY, **HELP!**
CHOMP!

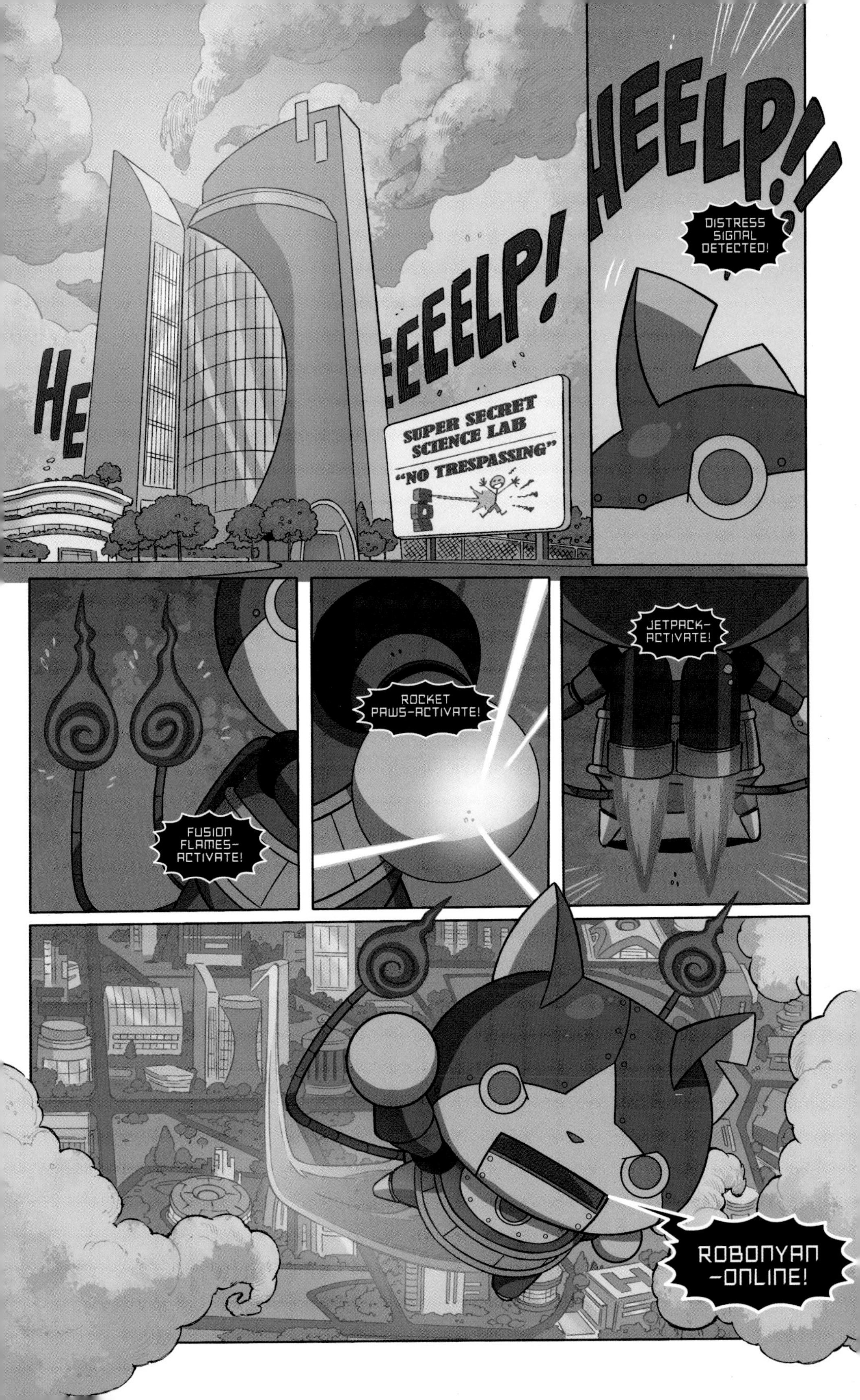

HEEEELP!
SUPER SECRET SCIENCE LAB
"NO TRESPASSING"
HEELP!!
DISTRESS SIGNAL DETECTED!
FUSION FLAMES—ACTIVATE!
ROCKET PAWS—ACTIVATE!
JETPACK—ACTIVATE!
ROBONYAN—ONLINE!

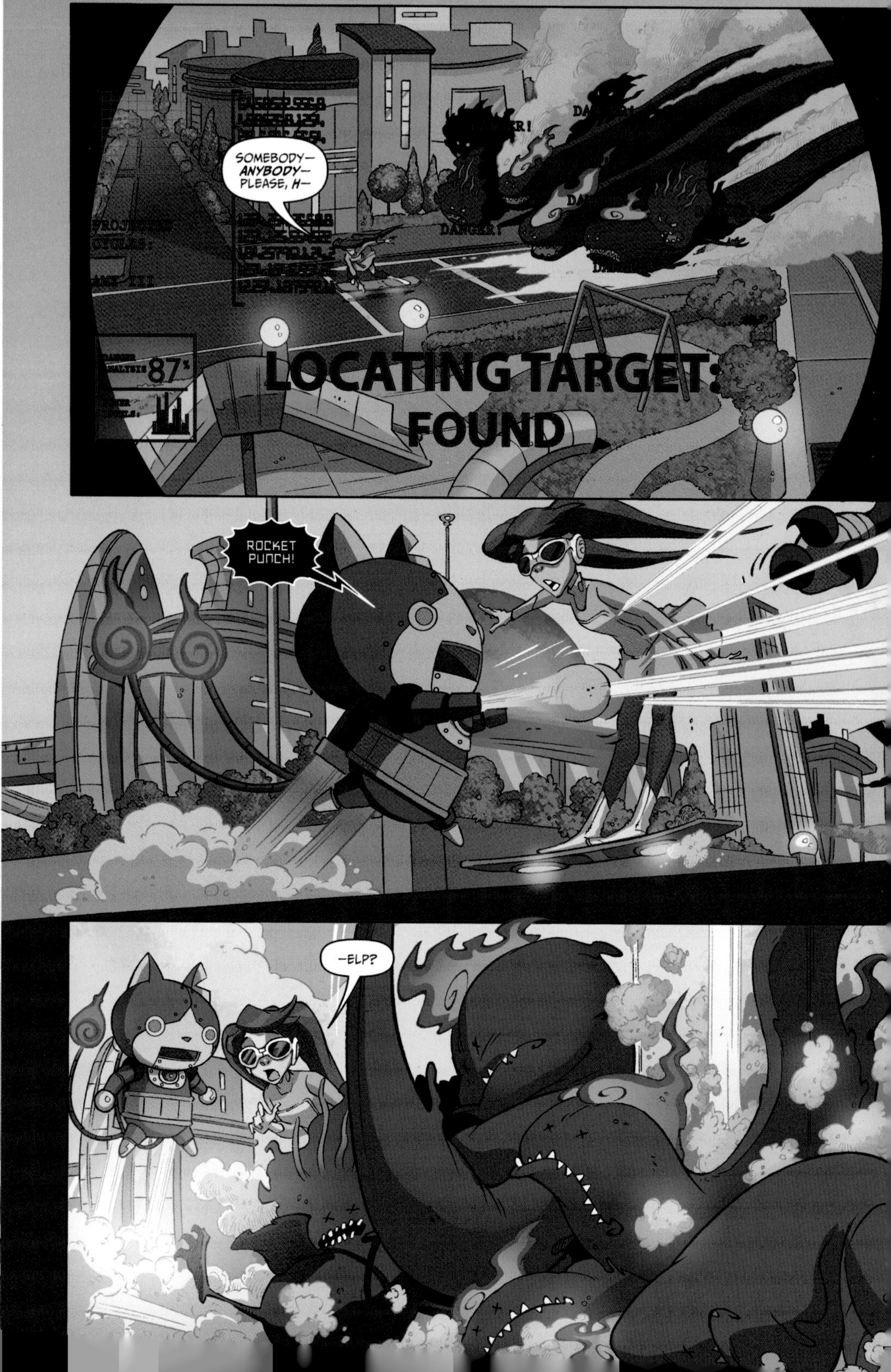
SOMEBODY—
ANYBODY—
PLEASE, H—
DANGER!
87%
LOCATING TARGET:
FOUND
ROCKET PUNCH!
—ELP?

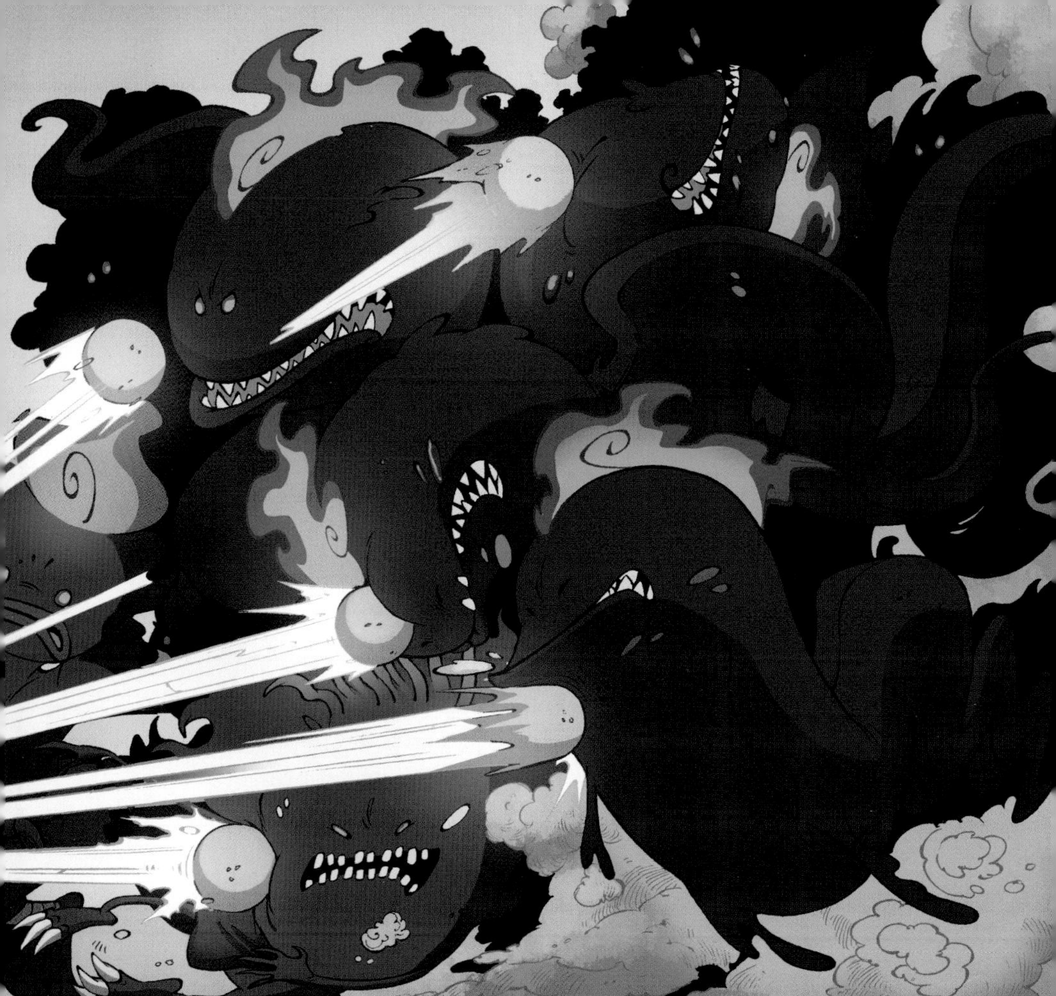

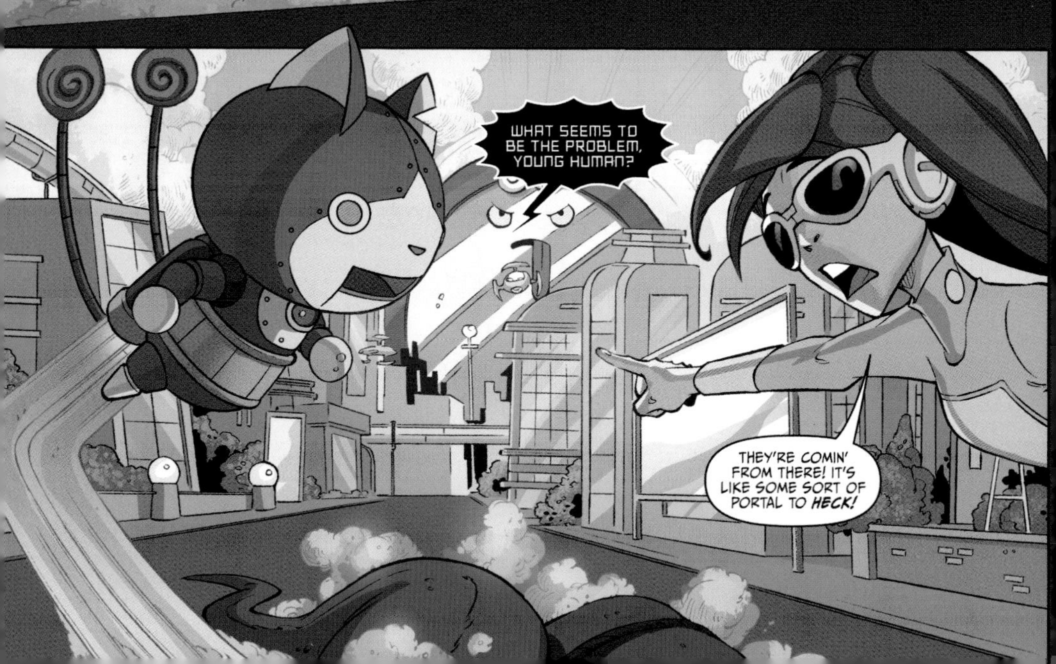
WHAT SEEMS TO BE THE PROBLEM, YOUNG HUMAN?
THEY'RE COMIN' FROM THERE! IT'S LIKE SOME SORT OF PORTAL TO ***HECK!***

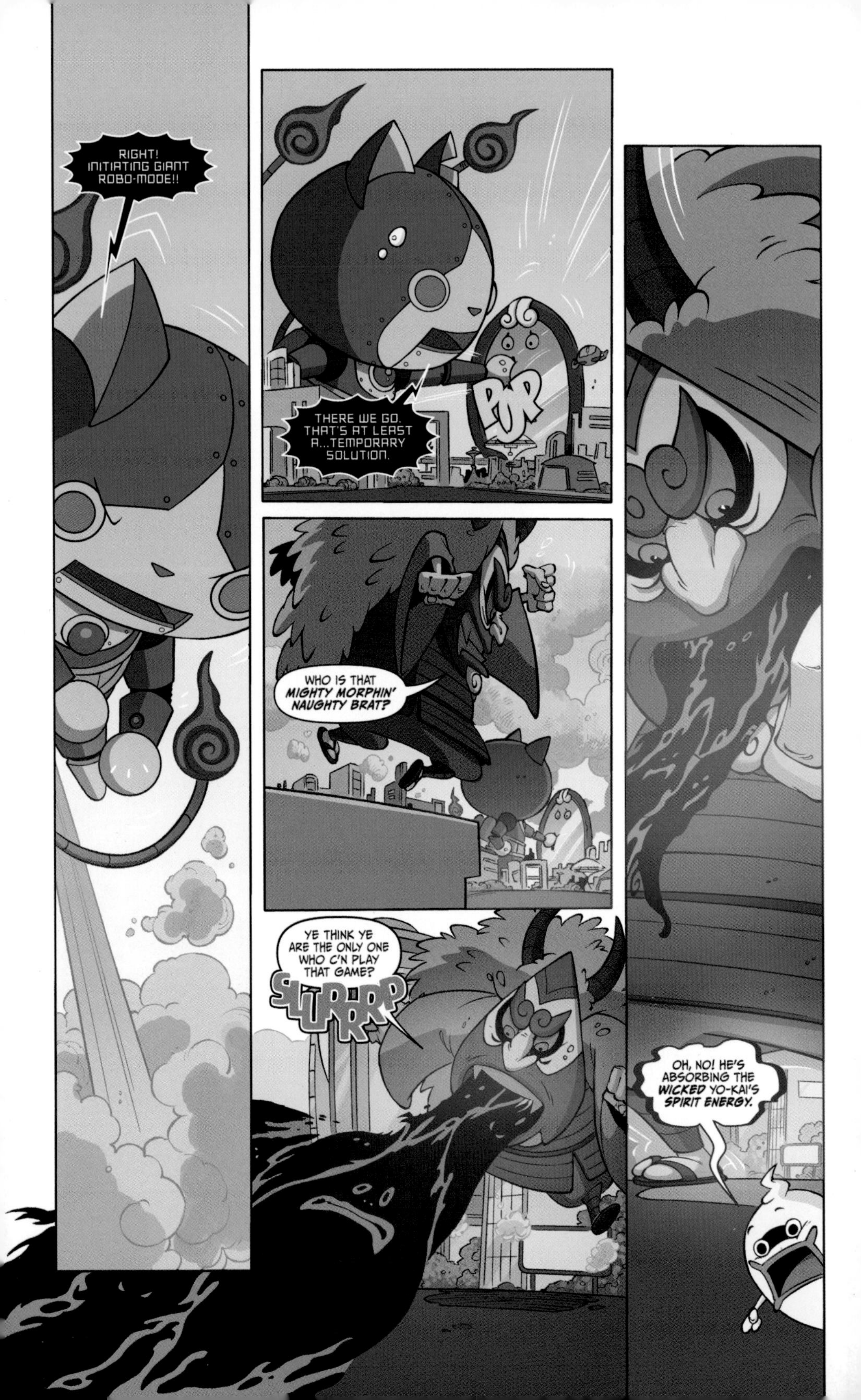
RIGHT! INITIATING GIANT ROBO-MODE!!
THERE WE GO. THAT'S AT LEAST A...TEMPORARY SOLUTION.
POP
WHO IS THAT MIGHTY MORPHIN' NAUGHTY BRAT?
YE THINK YE ARE THE ONLY ONE WHO C'N PLAY THAT GAME?
SLURRRRP
OH, NO! HE'S ABSORBING THE WICKED YO-KAI'S SPIRIT ENERGY.

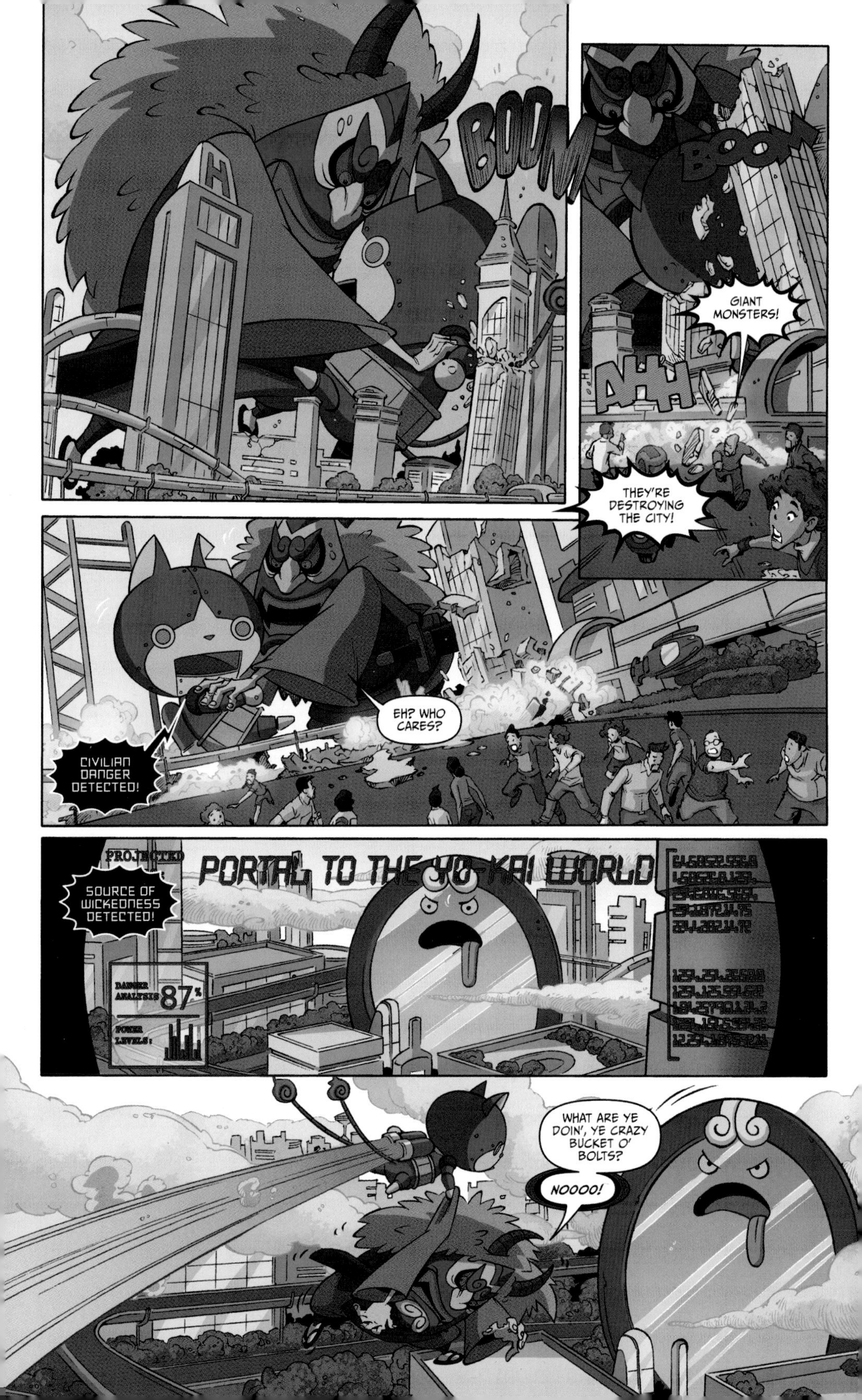
BOOM
BOOM
GIANT MONSTERS!
AHH
THEY'RE DESTROYING THE CITY!
EH? WHO CARES?
CIVILIAN DANGER DETECTED!
PROJECTED
PORTAL TO THE YO-KAI WORLD
SOURCE OF WICKEDNESS DETECTED!
DANGER ANALYSIS 87%
POWER LEVELS:
WHAT ARE YE DOIN', YE CRAZY BUCKET O' BOLTS?
NOOOO!

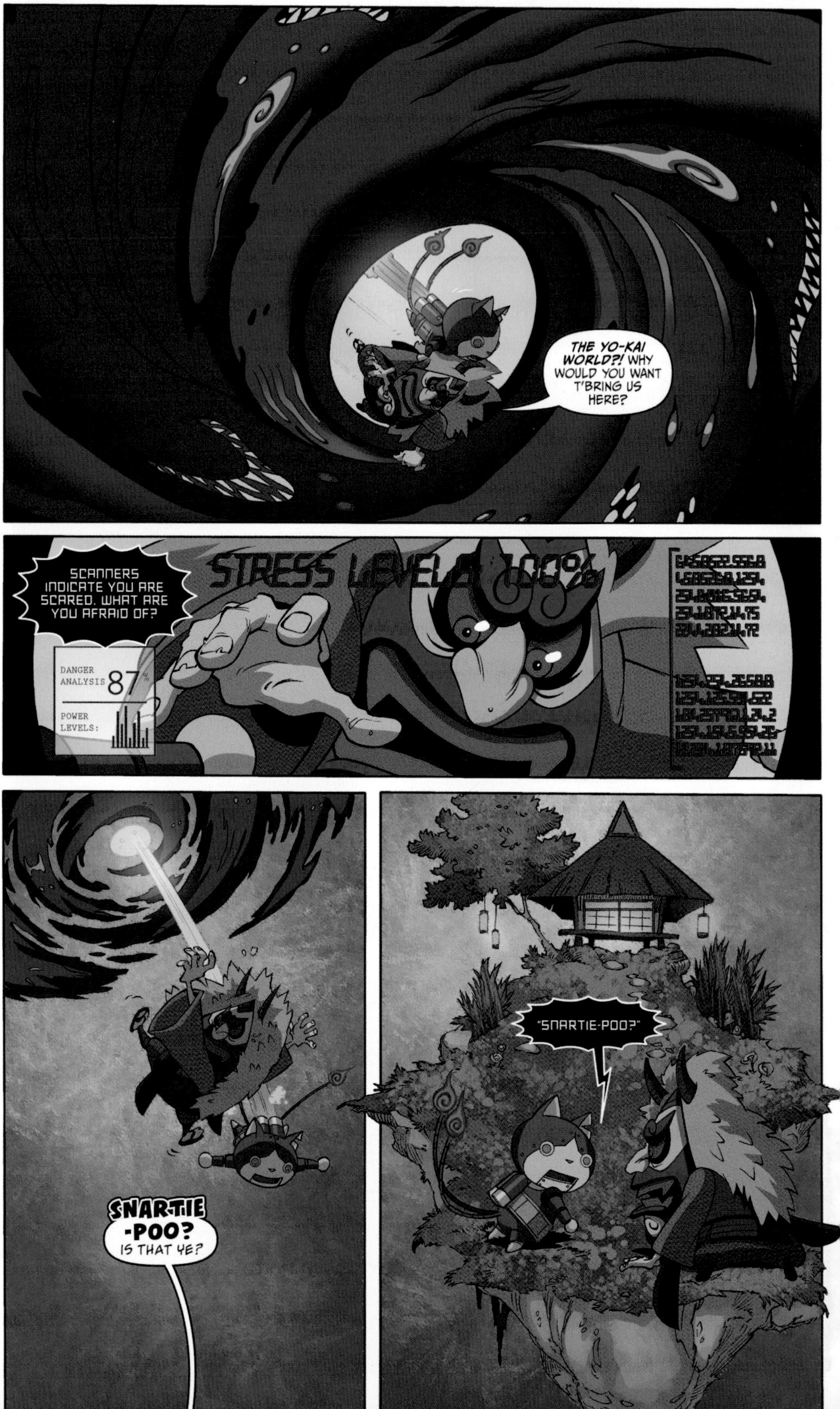
THE YO-KAI WORLD?! WHY WOULD YOU WANT T'BRING US HERE?
SCANNERS INDICATE YOU ARE SCARED. WHAT ARE YOU AFRAID OF?
STRESS LEVEL: 100%
DANGER ANALYSIS 87
POWER LEVELS:
SNARTIE -POO? IS THAT YE?
"SNARTIE-POO?"

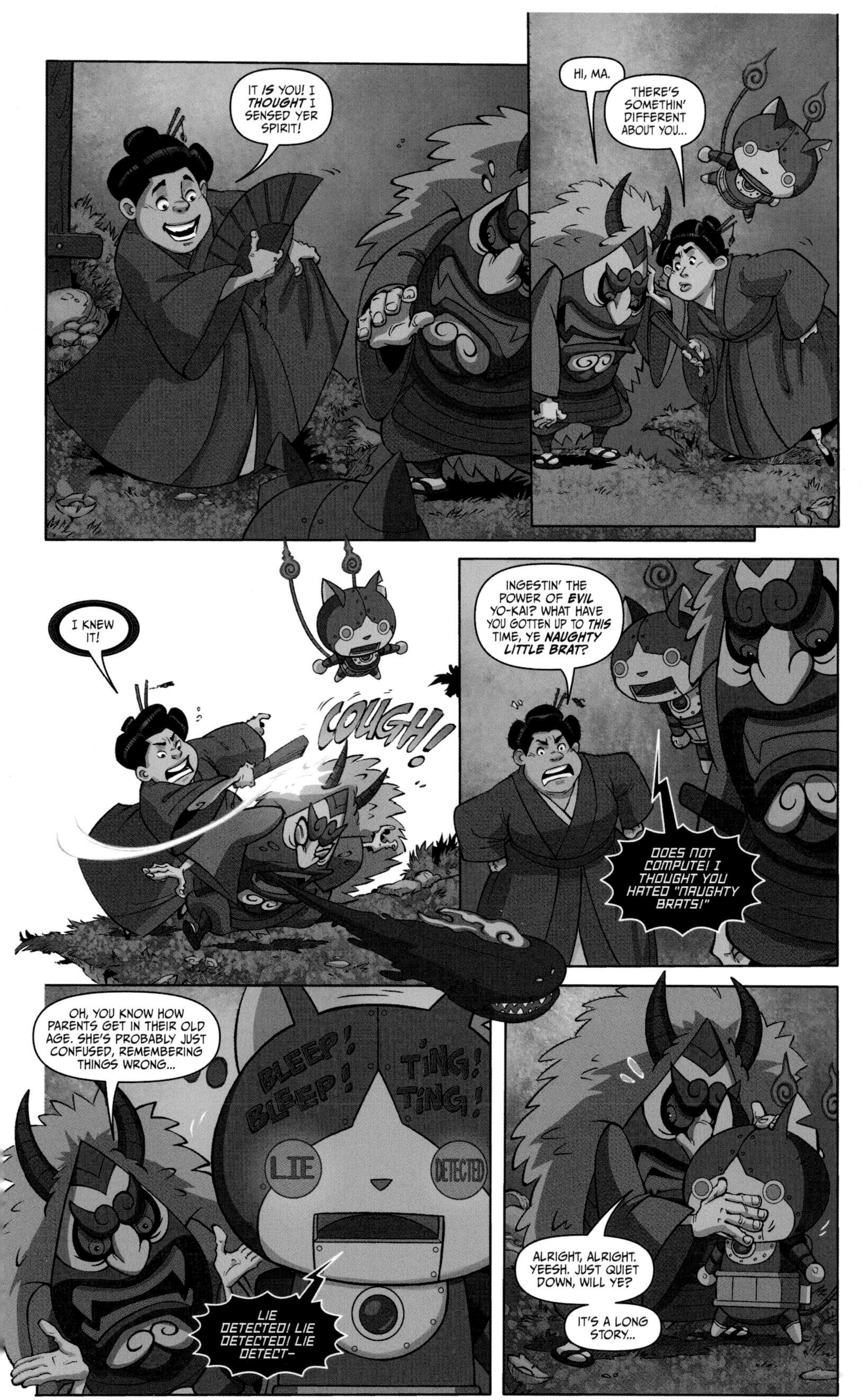
IT IS YOU! I THOUGHT I SENSED YER SPIRIT!
HI, MA.
THERE'S SOMETHIN' DIFFERENT ABOUT YOU...
I KNEW IT!
COUGH!
INGESTIN' THE POWER OF EVIL YO-KAI? WHAT HAVE YOU GOTTEN UP TO THIS TIME, YE NAUGHTY LITTLE BRAT?
DOES NOT COMPUTE! I THOUGHT YOU HATED "NAUGHTY BRATS!"
OH, YOU KNOW HOW PARENTS GET IN THEIR OLD AGE. SHE'S PROBABLY JUST CONFUSED, REMEMBERING THINGS WRONG...
BLEEP! BLEEP!
TING! TING!
LIE
DETECTED
LIE DETECTED! LIE DETECTED! LIE DETECT-
ALRIGHT, ALRIGHT. YEESH. JUST QUIET DOWN, WILL YE?
IT'S A LONG STORY...

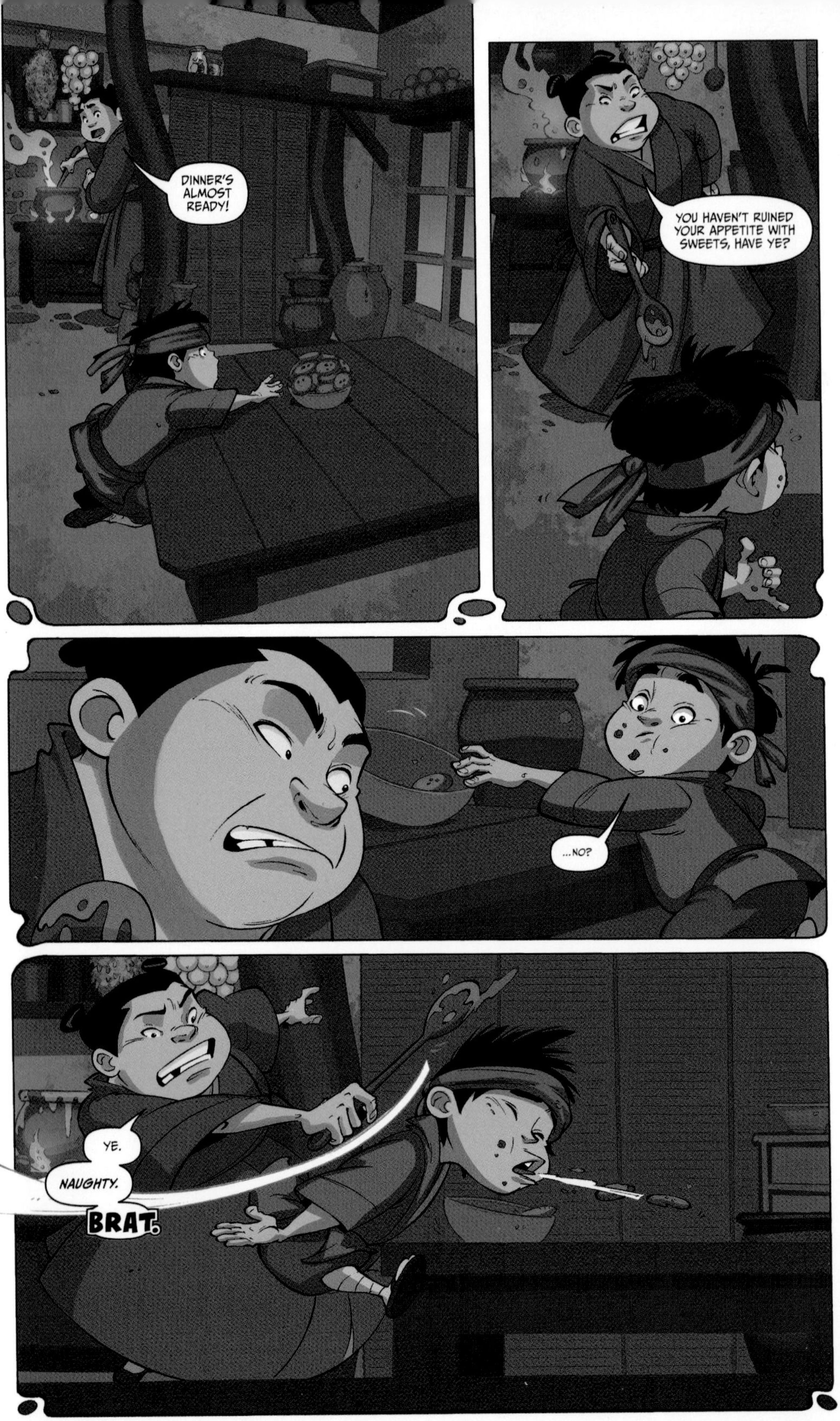
DINNER'S ALMOST READY!
YOU HAVEN'T RUINED YOUR APPETITE WITH SWEETS, HAVE YE?
...NO?
YE.
NAUGHTY.
BRAT.

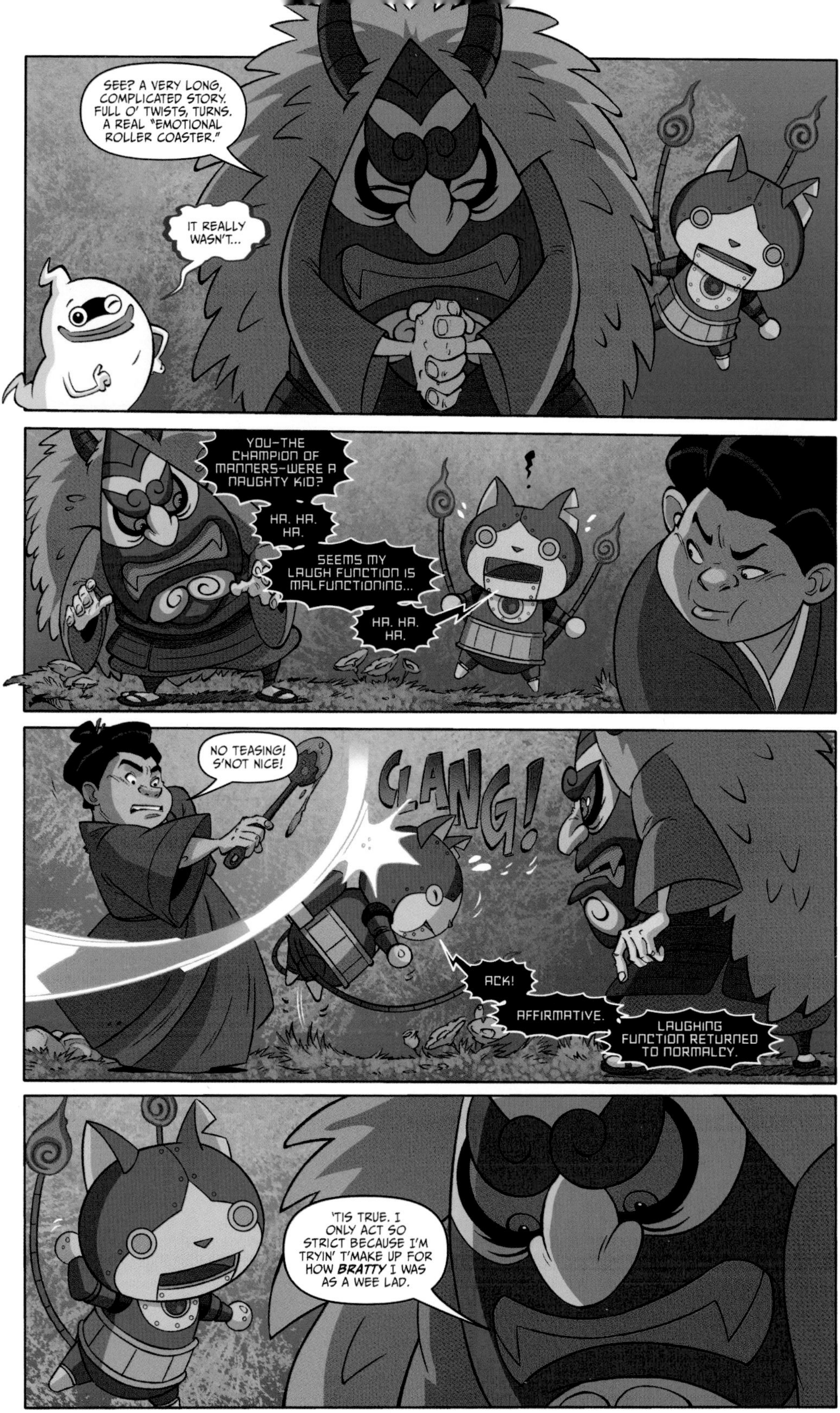
SEE? A VERY LONG, COMPLICATED STORY. FULL O' TWISTS, TURNS. A REAL "EMOTIONAL ROLLER COASTER."
IT REALLY WASN'T...
YOU–THE CHAMPION OF MANNERS–WERE A NAUGHTY KID?
HA. HA. HA.
SEEMS MY LAUGH FUNCTION IS MALFUNCTIONING...
HA. HA. HA.
NO TEASING! S'NOT NICE!
CLANG!
ACK!
AFFIRMATIVE.
LAUGHING FUNCTION RETURNED TO NORMALCY.
'TIS TRUE. I ONLY ACT SO STRICT BECAUSE I'M TRYIN' T'MAKE UP FOR HOW BRATTY I WAS AS A WEE LAD.

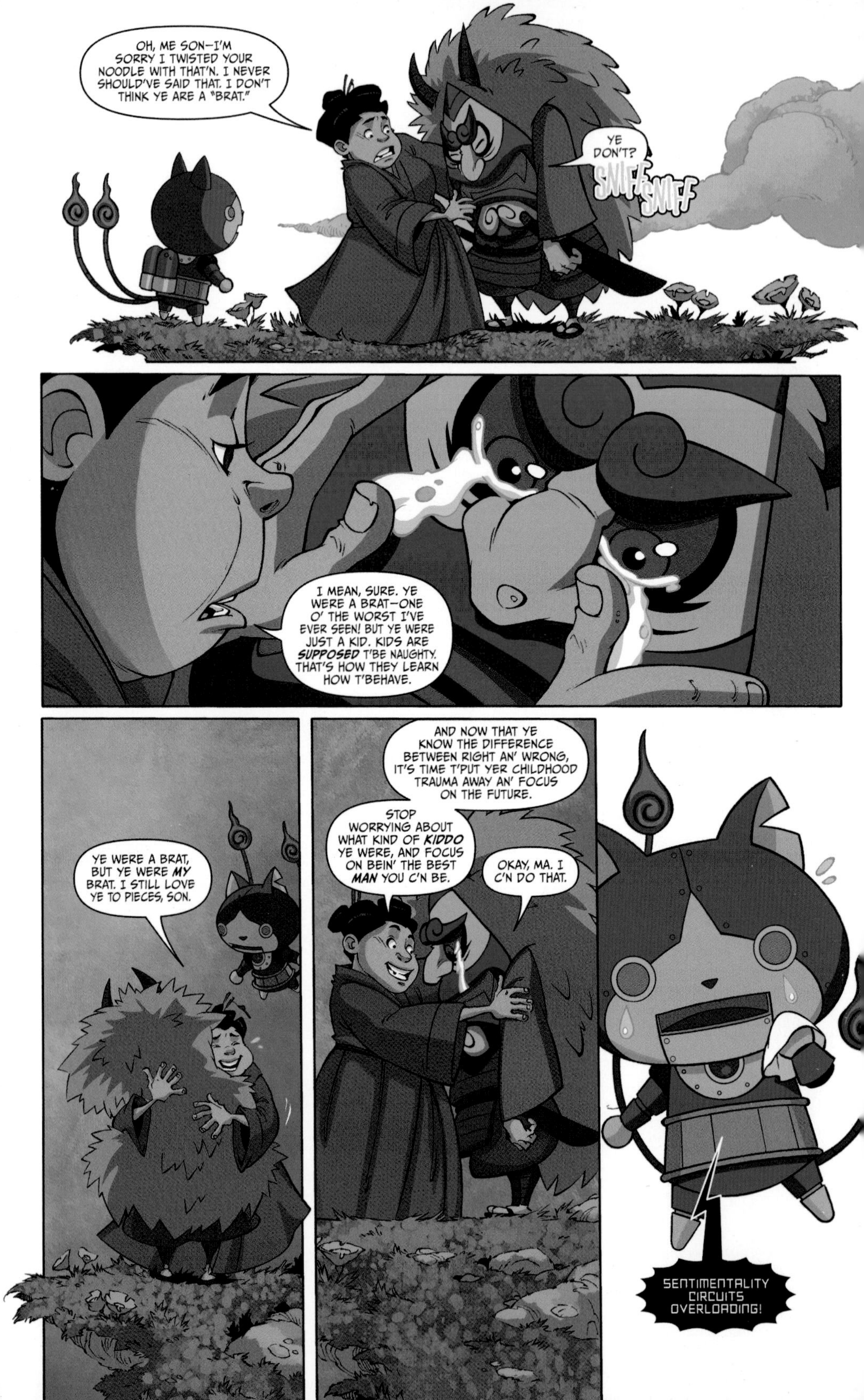
OH, ME SON—I'M SORRY I TWISTED YOUR NOODLE WITH THAT'N. I NEVER SHOULD'VE SAID THAT. I DON'T THINK YE ARE A "BRAT."
YE DON'T?
SNIFF SNIFF
I MEAN, SURE. YE WERE A BRAT—ONE O' THE WORST I'VE EVER SEEN! BUT YE WERE JUST A KID. KIDS ARE SUPPOSED T'BE NAUGHTY. THAT'S HOW THEY LEARN HOW T'BEHAVE.
YE WERE A BRAT, BUT YE WERE MY BRAT. I STILL LOVE YE TO PIECES, SON.
AND NOW THAT YE KNOW THE DIFFERENCE BETWEEN RIGHT AN' WRONG, IT'S TIME T'PUT YER CHILDHOOD TRAUMA AWAY AN' FOCUS ON THE FUTURE.
STOP WORRYING ABOUT WHAT KIND OF KIDDO YE WERE, AND FOCUS ON BEIN' THE BEST MAN YOU C'N BE.
OKAY, MA. I C'N DO THAT.
SENTIMENTALITY CIRCUITS OVERLOADING!

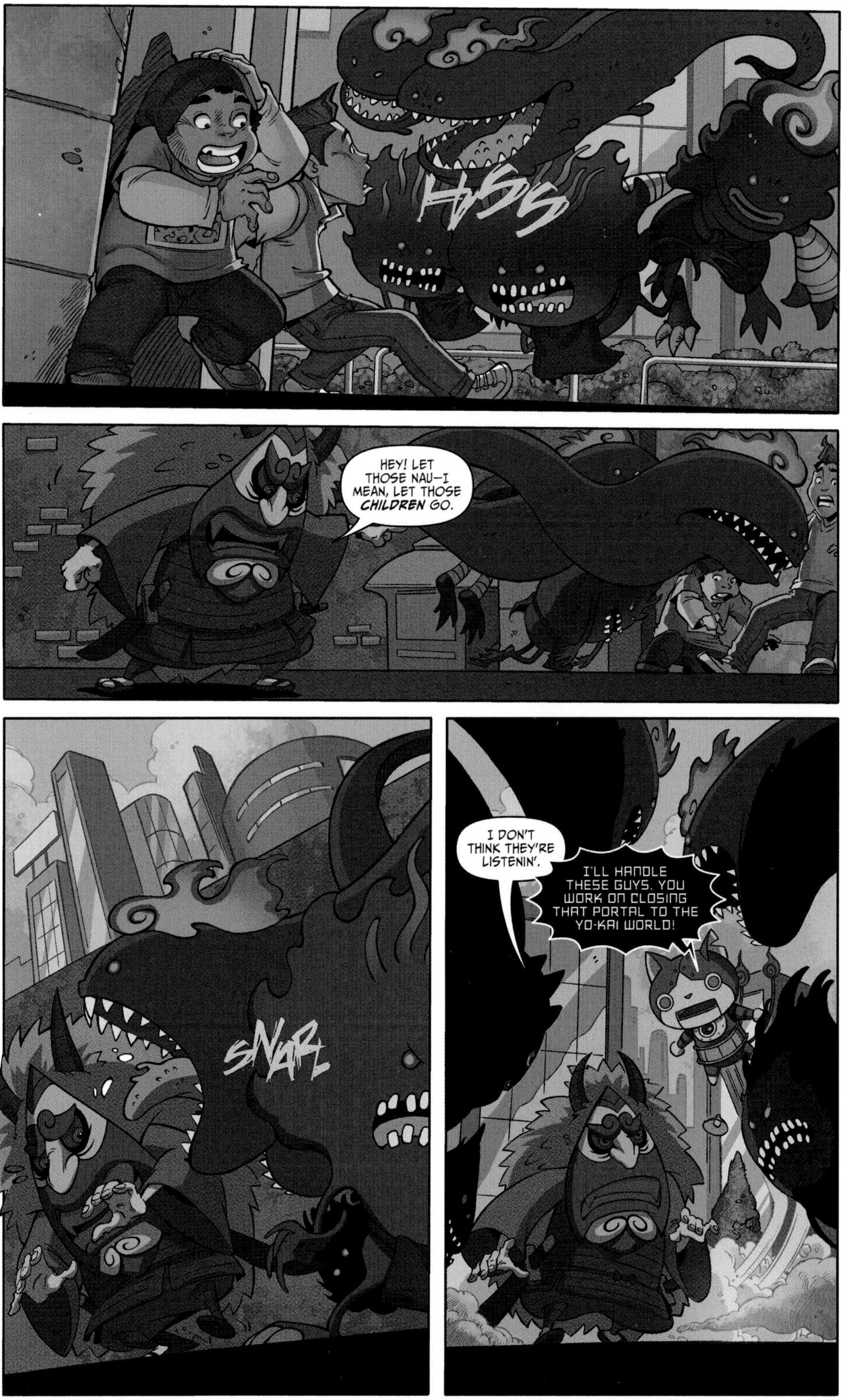
HISS
HEY! LET THOSE NAU—I MEAN, LET THOSE CHILDREN GO.
SNARL
I DON'T THINK THEY'RE LISTENIN'.
I'LL HANDLE THESE GUYS. YOU WORK ON CLOSING THAT PORTAL TO THE YO-KAI WORLD!

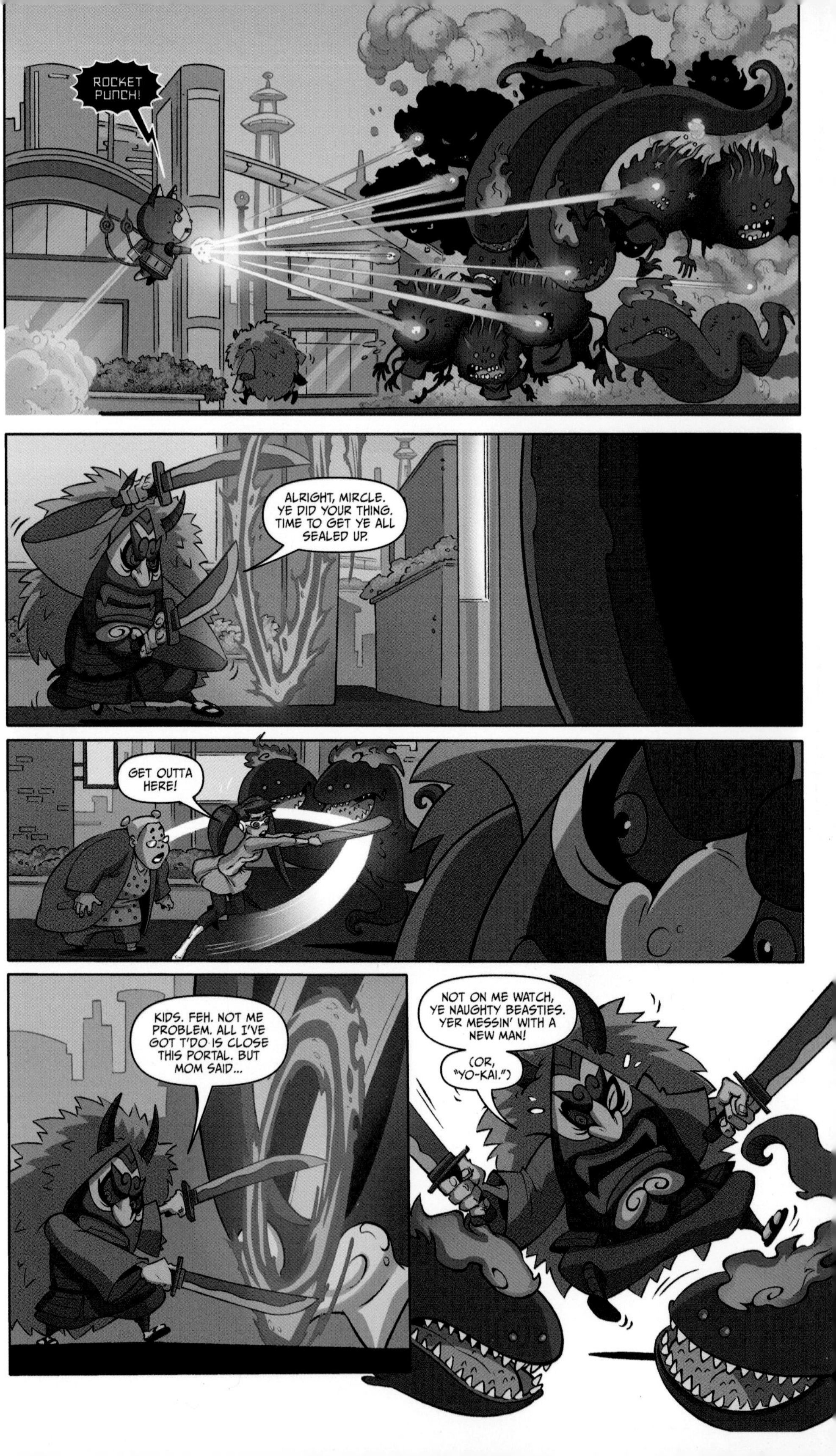
ROCKET PUNCH!
ALRIGHT, MIRCLE. YE DID YOUR THING. TIME TO GET YE ALL SEALED UP.
GET OUTTA HERE!
KIDS. FEH. NOT ME PROBLEM. ALL I'VE GOT T'DO IS CLOSE THIS PORTAL. BUT MOM SAID...
NOT ON ME WATCH, YE NAUGHTY BEASTIES. YER MESSIN' WITH A NEW MAN!
(OR, "YO-KAI.")

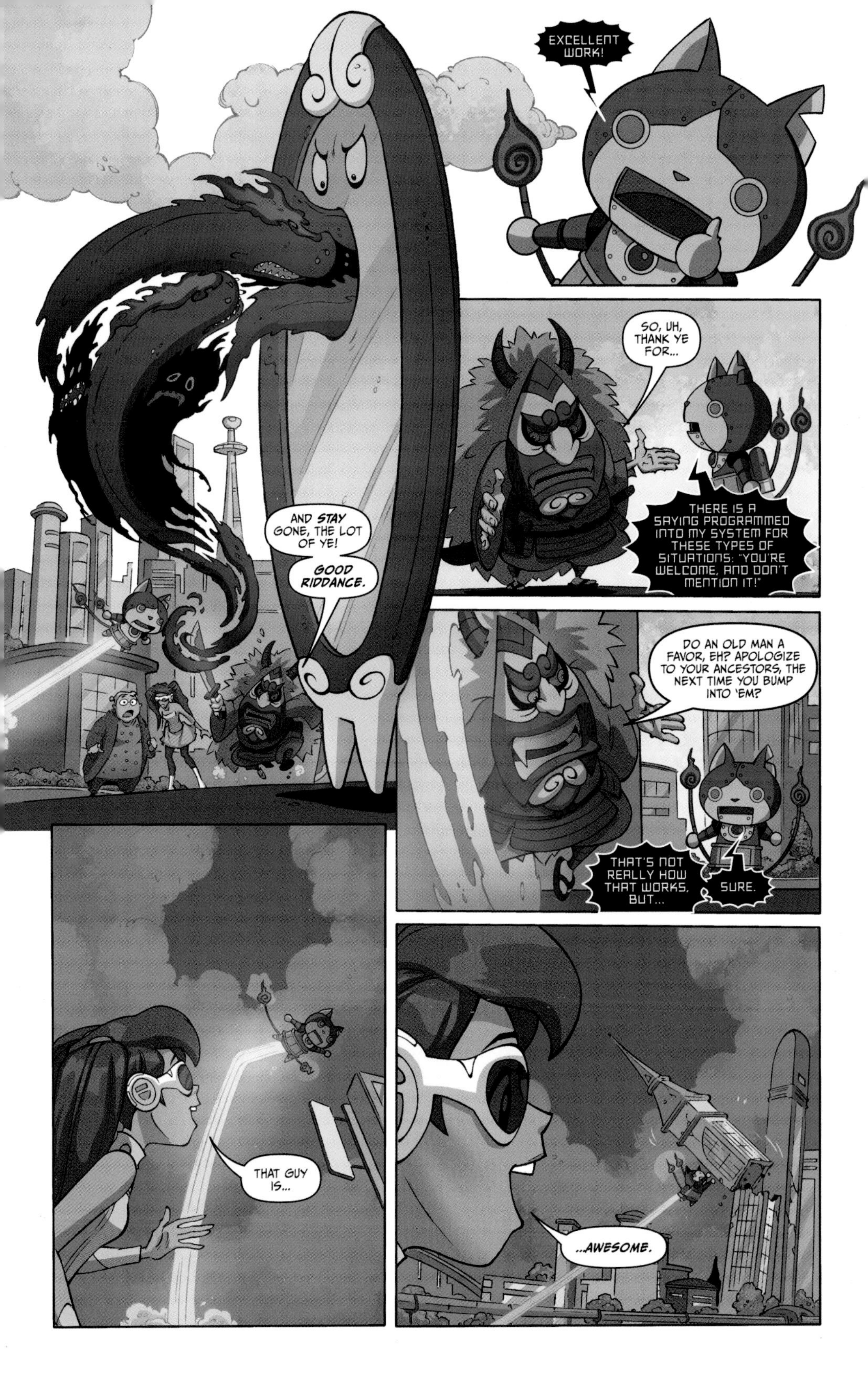
EXCELLENT WORK!
AND STAY GONE, THE LOT OF YE!
GOOD RIDDANCE.
SO, UH, THANK YE FOR...
THERE IS A SAYING PROGRAMMED INTO MY SYSTEM FOR THESE TYPES OF SITUATIONS: "YOU'RE WELCOME, AND DON'T MENTION IT!"
DO AN OLD MAN A FAVOR, EH? APOLOGIZE TO YOUR ANCESTORS, THE NEXT TIME YOU BUMP INTO 'EM?
THAT'S NOT REALLY HOW THAT WORKS, BUT...
SURE.
THAT GUY IS...
...AWESOME.

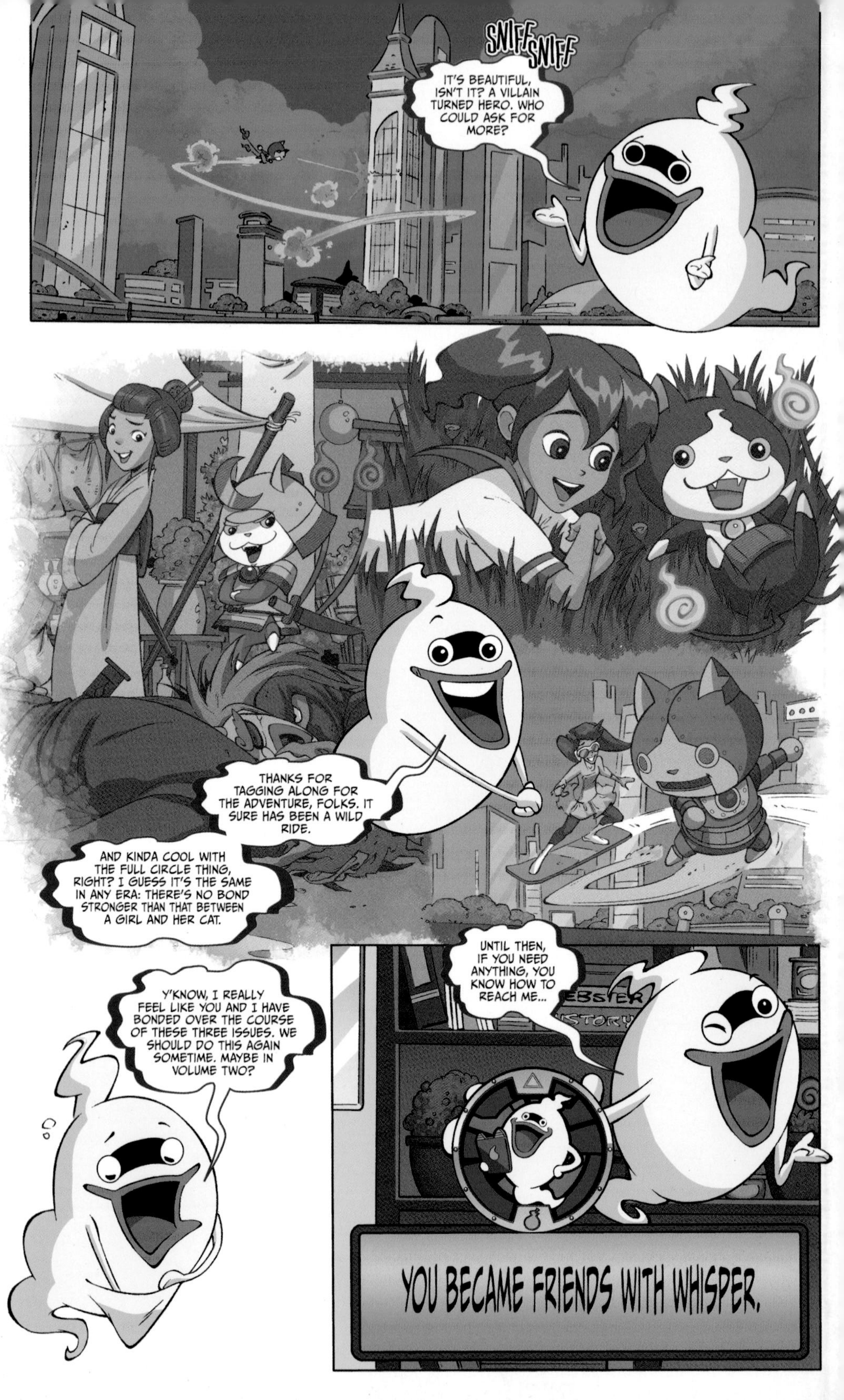

SNIFF SNIFF
IT'S BEAUTIFUL, ISN'T IT? A VILLAIN TURNED HERO. WHO COULD ASK FOR MORE?
THANKS FOR TAGGING ALONG FOR THE ADVENTURE, FOLKS. IT SURE HAS BEEN A WILD RIDE.
AND KINDA COOL WITH THE FULL CIRCLE THING, RIGHT? I GUESS IT'S THE SAME IN ANY ERA: THERE'S NO BOND STRONGER THAN THAT BETWEEN A GIRL AND HER CAT.
Y'KNOW, I REALLY FEEL LIKE YOU AND I HAVE BONDED OVER THE COURSE OF THESE THREE ISSUES. WE SHOULD DO THIS AGAIN SOMETIME. MAYBE IN VOLUME TWO?
UNTIL THEN, IF YOU NEED ANYTHING, YOU KNOW HOW TO REACH ME...
YOU BECAME FRIENDS WITH WHISPER.

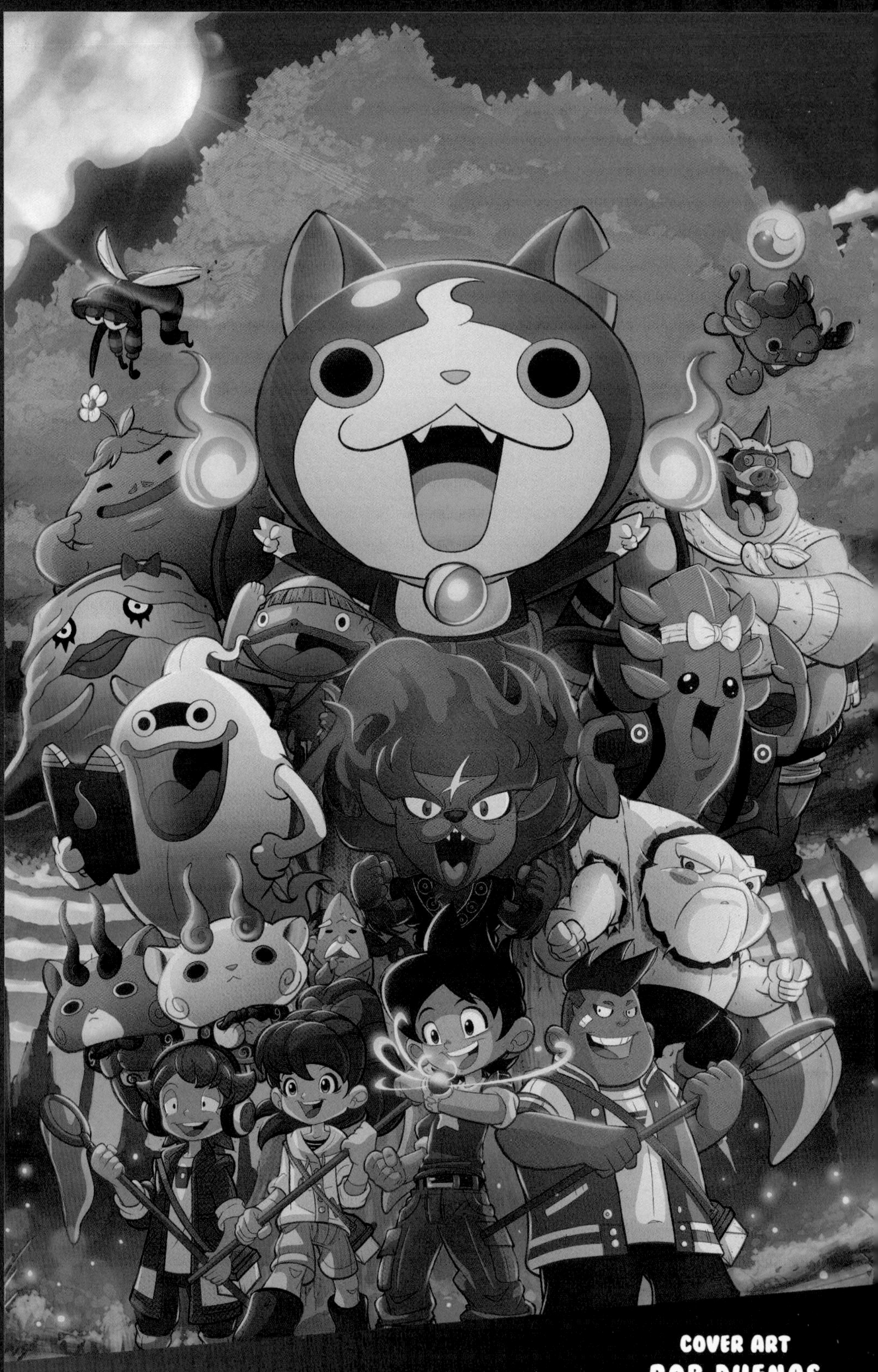

COVER ART
ROB DUENAS

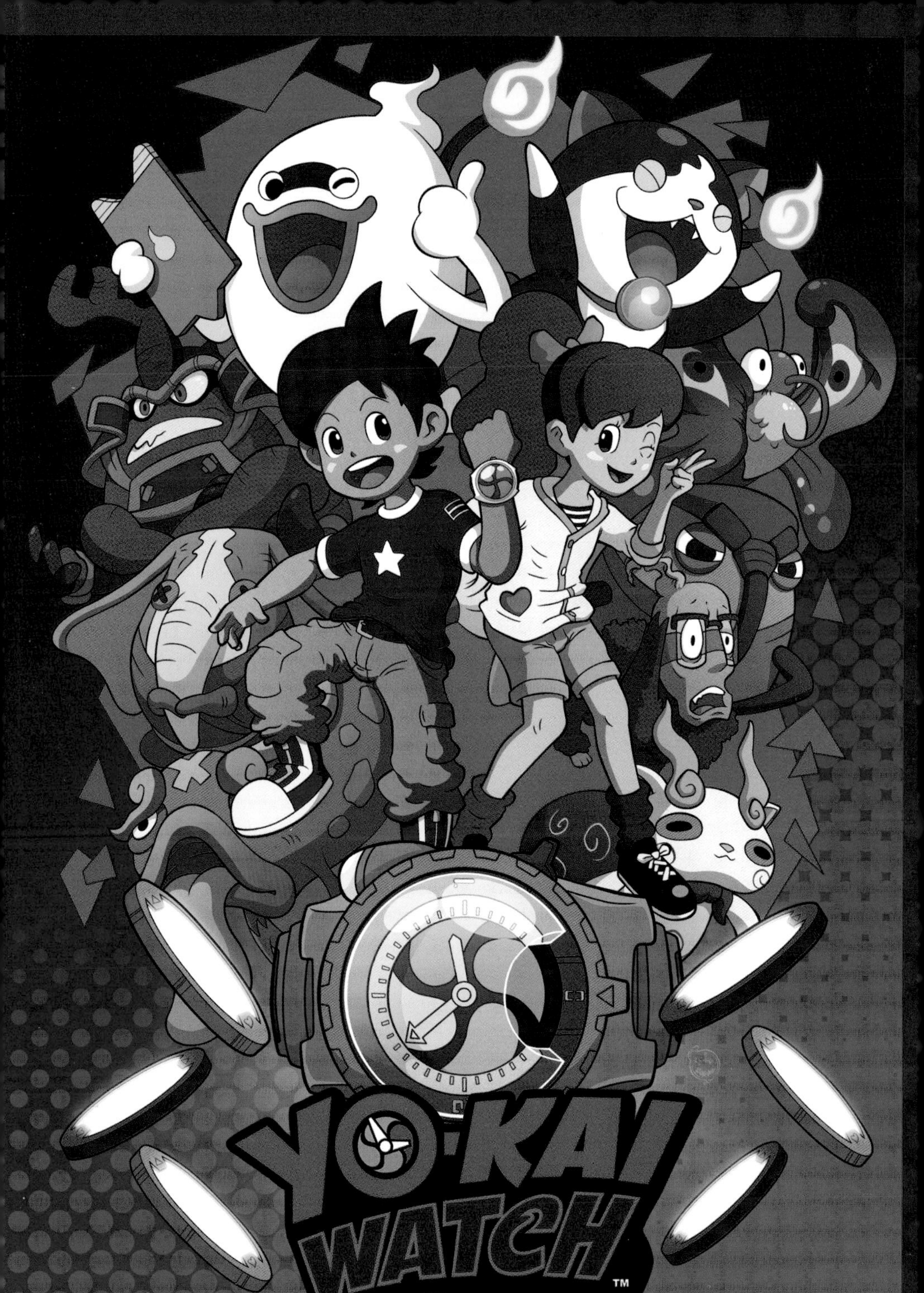
YO-KAI
WATCH™

COVER ART
PHILIP MURPHY

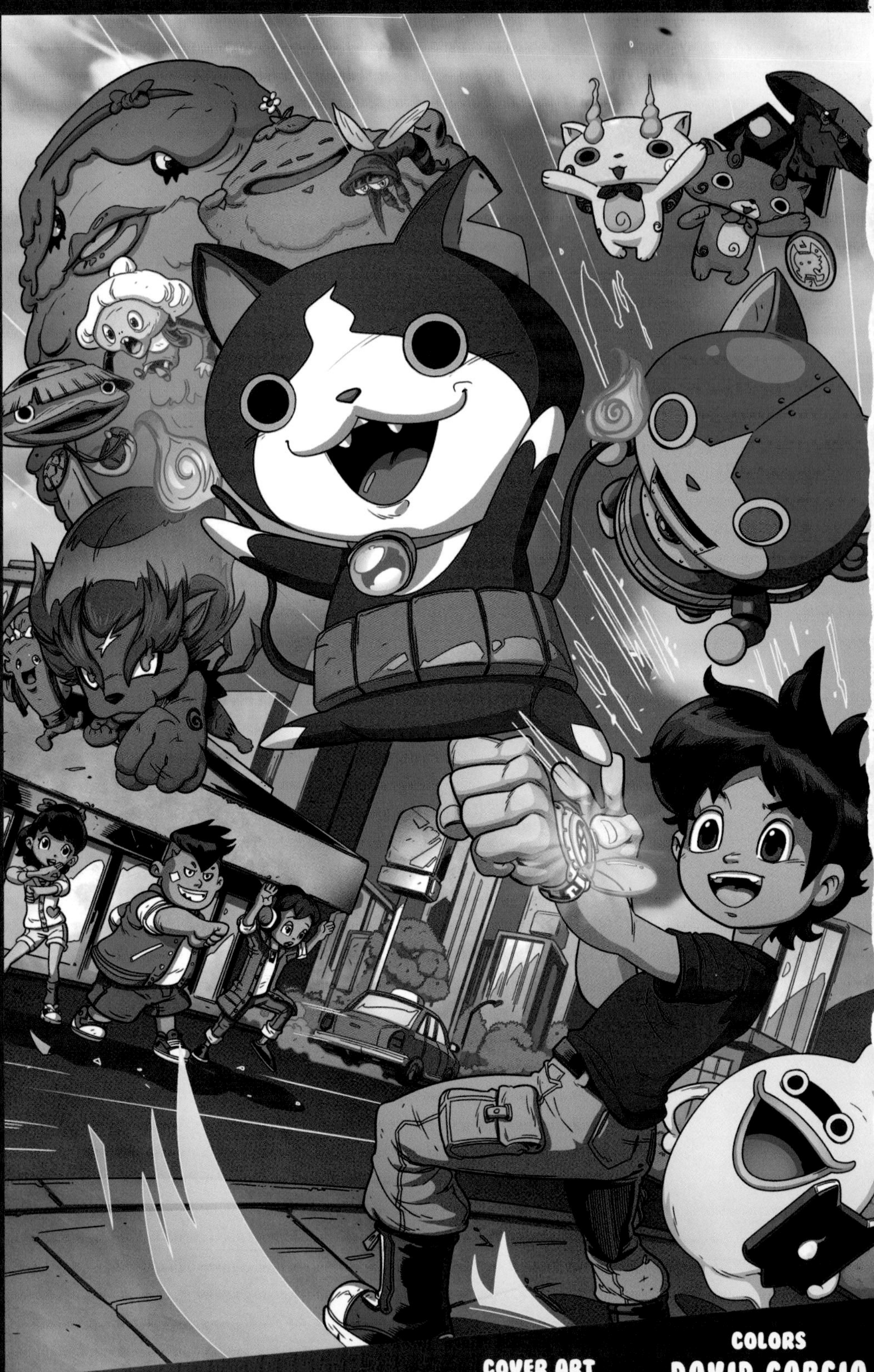

COVER ART
FICO OSSIO

COLORS
DAVID GARCIA
CRUZ